TIM FRAZER
AND THE
MELYNFFOREST MYSTERY

Francis Durbridge

WILLIAMS & WHITING

Cover design by Timo Schroeder

9781915887108

Williams & Whiting (Publishers)

15 Chestnut Grove, Hurstpierpoint,

West Sussex, BN6 9SS

Titles by Francis Durbridge published by Williams & Whiting

1   The Scarf – tv serial
2   Paul Temple and the Curzon Case – radio serial
3   La Boutique – radio serial
4   The Broken Horseshoe – tv serial
5   Three Plays for Radio Volume 1
6   Send for Paul Temple – radio serial
7   A Time of Day – tv serial
8   Death Comes to The Hibiscus – stage play
    The Essential Heart – radio play
    (writing as Nicholas Vane)
9   Send for Paul Temple – stage play
10 The Teckman Biography – tv serial
11 Paul Temple and Steve – radio serial
12 Twenty Minutes From Rome – a teleplay
13 Portrait of Alison – tv serial
14 Paul Temple: Two Plays for Radio Volume 1
15 Three Plays for Radio Volume 2
16 The Other Man – tv serial
17 Paul Temple and the Spencer Affair – radio serial
18 Step In The Dark – film script
19 My Friend Charles – tv serial
20 A Case For Paul Temple – radio serial
21 Murder In The Media – more rediscovered serials and
    stories
22 The Desperate People – tv serial
23 Paul Temple: Two Plays for Television
24 And Anthony Sherwood Laughed – radio series
25 The World of Tim Frazer – tv serial
26 Paul Temple Intervenes – radio serial
27 Passport To Danger! – radio serial
28 Bat Out of Hell – tv serial
29 Send For Paul Temple Again – radio serial
30 Mr Hartington Died Tomorrow – radio serial

Murder At The Weekend – the rediscovered newspaper serials and short stories

Also published by Williams & Whiting:
Francis Durbridge : The Complete Guide
By Melvyn Barnes

Titles by Francis Durbridge to be published by Williams & Whiting

Murder On The Continent (Further re-discovered serials and stories)

News of Paul Temple

Operation Diplomat

Paul Temple and the Alex Affair

Paul Temple and the Canterbury Case (film script)

Paul Temple and the Conrad Case

Paul Temple and the Geneva Mystery

Paul Temple and the Margo Mystery

Paul Temple: Two Plays For Radio Vol 2 (Send For Paul Temple and News of Paul Temple)

The Passenger

INTRODUCTION

Francis Durbridge (1912-98) was the foremost writer of mystery thrillers for BBC radio from the 1930s to the 1960s. As early as 1938 he found the niche in which he was to establish his name, when his serial *Send for Paul Temple* was so successful that it resulted in numerous sequels that built an impressive UK and European fanbase. Then later, while continuing to write for radio, he decided to move into television – with the result that in 1952 *The Broken Horseshoe* became the first thriller serial on BBC Television.

The World of Tim Frazer was Durbridge's ninth television serial, and while his previous eight had each consisted of six thirty-minute episodes this one ran for eighteen thirty-minute episodes covering three stories. Transmitted from 15 November 1960 to 14 March 1961, it was the longest serial yet shown on BBC Television, and it qualified as continuous by using the audience-holding technique of a cliff-hanger ending to each episode but with the changeover in stories taking place during episodes seven and thirteen. Although Durbridge originally planned to use the title *The World of David Marquand*, the change to Tim Frazer cemented the latter's place in television history.

From the first Tim Frazer serial, written jointly with Clive Exton, it was clear that Frazer was a totally different character from radio's Paul Temple - an ordinary man lacking Temple's sophistication, and with no intention of becoming a detective until drawn into the counter-espionage game. The second serial, *The Salinger Affair*, was written jointly with Barry Thomas and Charles Hatton; while for the third, *The Melynfforest Mystery*, Durbridge was again joined by co-writers Thomas and Hatton.

All three inter-linked Tim Frazer serials featured superb performances by Jack Hedley (1929-2021) as Tim and Ralph Michael (1907-94) as his spymaster Charles Ross.

While Hedley had appeared regularly on television in the 1950s, his role as Frazer enhanced his reputation and led to film and television successes – including the Hammer films *The Scarlet Blade* (1963) and *The Anniversary* (1968), television's *Colditz* (1972-74) and *Who Pays the Ferryman?* (1977), and the James Bond movie *For Your Eyes Only* (1981). His Durbridge credentials also became established, as he appeared in the *Paul Temple* television series (*Murder in Munich*, 12 and 19 July 1970) and also in the 1983 UK tour of Durbridge's stage play *Nightcap*.

European television companies produced the three Tim Frazer serials separately, rather than in a continuous sequence. The first was screened in Germany as *Tim Frazer* (14 – 25 January 1963, six episodes), translated by Marianne de Barde and directed by Hans Quest; and the Italian version was *Traffico d'armi nel golfo* (12 – 26 November 1977, three episodes), translated by Franca Cancogni, adapted by Aurelio Chiesa and directed by Leonardo Cortese. The second serial appeared in Germany as *Tim Frazer – Der Fall Salinger* (10 – 20 January 1964, six episodes), translated by Marianne de Barde and directed by Hans Quest; and in France as *La mort d'un touriste* (3 October – 7 November 1975, six episodes), translated and directed by Abder Isker.

But the third Frazer serial, *The Melynfforest Mystery*, did not reach German television screens for some years. *Das Messer* (30 November – 4 December 1971, three episodes), translated by Marianne de Barde and directed by Rolf von Sydow, was the product of considerable re-writing – involving not only new characters (Tim Frazer became Jim Ellis and Charles Ross became George Baker) but changes to the plot that even saw the revelation of a different guilty party.

Durbridge was himself involved in this German production some ten years after his original UK serial, and there is an interesting connection with the fact that he annually listed in his *Who's Who* entry a 1971 television serial entitled *Stupid like a Fox*. Indeed, on 1 September 1970 the newspaper *Hamburger Abendblatt* reported that Rolf von Sydow was to direct a new Durbridge serial called *Dumm wie ein Fuchs* (*Stupid like a Fox*) for transmission in 1971. But now it is known that this was intended to be a German version of Durbridge's latest UK television serial *The Passenger*, whereas the German producers insisted on proceeding instead with a new Tim Frazer translation, *Das Messer*.

The World of Tim Frazer was novelised, but with each of the three serials becoming a separate book. *The World of Tim Frazer* (Hodder & Stoughton, January 1962) was also published in the US in August 1962 by Dodd, Mead. In Germany it appeared as *Tim Frazer*, in France as *Où est passé Harry?* and in the Netherlands as *De wereld van Tim Frazer*. For English-speaking lovers of audiobooks, there were audiocassettes and CDs read by Clive Mantle (BBC Audio, 2009) and later on CDs there was an abridged reading by Anthony Head (AudioGO, 2010). The second serial became *Tim Frazer Again* (Hodder & Stoughton, March 1964), published in Germany as *Tim Frazer und der Fall Salinger*, in France as *Le Rendez-vous de sept heures trente* and in Portugal as *O Caso Salinger*. Again audiobook fans were provided with CDs of an abridged reading by Anthony Head (AudioGO, 2011) and a complete reading by Clive Mantle (AudioGO, 2012) as an audio download that does not appear to be available on CDs. The third serial was much later novelised as *Tim Frazer Gets the Message* (Hodder & Stoughton, November 1978), and in Germany as *Tim Frazer weiß Bescheid*. This time audio fans again had CDs with an abridged reading by Anthony Head (AudioGO, 2011) and a complete reading by Clive Mantle (AudioGO, 2012).

Tim Frazer only appeared once on cinema screens, in the Austrian film *Tim Frazer jagt den geheimnisvollen Mister X* ("Tim Frazer Chasing the Mysterious Mister X"). This was made by Melba Film Wien in 1964, and was also released in Belgium as *Tim Frazer à la poursuite du mystérieux Monsieur X*, in Italy as *Tim Frazer caccia il misterioso Mister X* and in the USA *as Case 33: Antwerp*. It was directed by Ernst Hofbauer, who also wrote the screenplay from a story by Anton van Casteren; and although Durbridge was credited on the film's poster and trailer as the creator of Tim Frazer, he received no acknowledgement on the film itself. Indeed Durbridge had no direct involvement in this film.

Very recently, however, a typescript was found in Durbridge's archives entitled *Tim Frazer and the Melvin Affair*, which is now included as a bonus in this volume. It is a film scenario, but there is no evidence that the film was ever produced. There is no date on it, but obviously it must have been written later than the 1960/61 television serials – and Durbridge, ever the consummate re-cycler, this time revived the plot of his 1945 radio serial *Passport to Danger!*

Melvyn Barnes
Author of *Francis Durbridge: The Complete Guide* (Williams & Whiting, 2018)

This book reproduces Francis Durbridge's original script together with the list of characters and actors of the BBC programme on the dates mentioned, but the eventual broadcast might have edited Durbridge's script in respect of scenes, dialogue and character names.

TIM FRAZER
AND THE
MELYNFFOREST MYSTERY

A serial in six episodes
By FRANCIS DURBRIDGE,
BARRY THOMAS & CHARLES HATTON

Broadcast on BBC Television
Feb 7th 1961 – 14th March 1961

CAST:

Tim Frazer . . . . Jack Hedley
Charles Ross . . . . .Ralph Michael
Hobson . . . . Howell Evans
Chief Supt Nash . . . . Martin Boddey
Major Lockwood . . . . Jack Watling
Miss Thackeray . . . . .Ellen McIntosh
Edward Jones . . . . Edward Palmer
Davy Williams . . . . .Prysor Williams
Mrs Crichton . . . . .Hazel Hughes
Elwyn Roberts . . . . .Laurence Hardy
Roger Thornton . . . . .David Langton
Dr Norman Vincent . . . . Walter Horsbrugh
Eddie Davies . . . . .Douglas Blackwell
Phone Operator . . . . Branwen Iorweth
Det Insp Royd . . . . John Glyn-Jones
Det Sgt Owen . . . . .Alan Stuart
Fred . . . . Meurig Wyn-Jones
Stan White . . . . David Lander
Laurence James . . . . Patrick McAlinney
Constable Hughes . . . . Edward Brooks
Chief Constable . . . . Ballard Berkeley
Rita Colman . . . . Helen Lindsay
Kurt Lander . . . . John Stevenson Lang

Tug Wallis . . . . Colin Douglas
Al Cross . . . . Murray Evans
A Doctor . . . . .Robert Croudace
A youth . . . . John Pike
Captain Stribling . . . . Thomas Gallagher
A girl . . . . Balbina

Other parts played by
Robert Brown, Richard Holden,
Richard Pescud, Peter Layton,
Clive Pollitt, Robert Pitt, Noel Barrow,
and Heather Downham

EPISODE ONE

OPEN TO: The Library, 29 Smith Square. Day.

CHARLES ROSS is sitting at his desk writing a letter. He pauses to take a sip of coffee occasionally. HOBSON, a civil servant, enters with several files which he places on the desk.

HOBSON: Excuse me, sir. Chief Superintendent Nash is waiting to see you.

ROSS: (*Vaguely*) Nash?

HOBSON: The Assistant Commissioner telephoned on Monday to make the appointment.

ROSS: (*Thoughtfully*) Oh, yes, that's right, Hobson – he did. Show the Superintendent in.

HOBSON nods and goes out.

ROSS puts aside the letter and rises to meet NASH as HOBSON shows him in.

HOBSON: Superintendent Nash, sir.

ROSS: Good morning.

NASH: Good morning, Mr Ross. It's very good of you to see me.

HOBSON retires at a signal from ROSS. ROSS indicates the armchair facing the desk to NASH.

ROSS: Sit down, Superintendent. What can I do for you?

NASH: I don't know whether Sir Thomas told you why …

ROSS: (*Shaking his head*) He simply said you wanted to see me – that it was something to do with a murder case.

NASH: That's right. The Melynfforest Case.

NASH passes a newspaper to ROSS. ROSS looks at the newspaper, reading the account of the murder. NASH watches him.

ROSS: (*Looking up*) This seems a very unpleasant business. They seem to be hinting that you've come up against a blank wall.

NASH: We have, sir.

ROSS: Well, I'm sorry. But I don't quite see why Sir Thomas should suggest …

NASH: He didn't suggest anything. This is entirely my idea, sir – coming to see you.

ROSS: Go on, Superintendent.

NASH: I thought there was a chance, just a slim chance, that you might have heard of Elaine Bradford.

ROSS: The murdered woman?

NASH: Yes. It's fifteen days now since we found her body in that wood – face battered in until it was almost unrecognisable. A harmless sort of woman – no apparent motive …

ROSS: (*Thoughtfully*) Melynfforest, that's in Wales – near Seaguard.

NASH: (*Nodding*) About ten miles away … All right for holidays. Not so good for murder investigation. The people talk to everybody except the police. Not that Miss Bradford had any background in those parts – she'd only been there ten days. She was staying at a guest house run by a Mrs Crichton.

ROSS: Didn't she make any friends in the village?

NASH: A few, but she never gave anything away about her past life. Seems she'd travelled abroad a lot and wasn't short of money. We got that from an estate agent named Roger Thornton. She had ideas of buying a cottage from him.

ROSS: I see.

NASH: Apparently, she wasn't very easy to please – according to Thornton he'd showed her every property on his books.

ROSS: (*Looking at the newspaper*) And that's all you know about her?

NASH: Yes. No notice, no suspects, no background. She was in her mid-forties and seemed to get on with most people. Though some of them thought she was a bit of a mystery woman.

ROSS: I can imagine that – in a Welsh village!

NASH: There's something very odd about this case, Mr Ross – very odd.

ROSS: Well, the odd thing so far as I am concerned is why you should have consulted me.

NASH: I had a hunch, sir.

ROSS: What kind of a hunch?

NASH: (*After a momentary hesitation*) I wondered if, by any chance, Miss Bradford was working for your department?

ROSS: Oh! (*Faintly amused*) Oh – now I get the point! Now I see what you're getting at! (*Shaking his head*) I'm sorry to disappoint you. We have no agents in the Principality – not even among the Welsh Nationalists!

NASH rises and holds out his hand.

NASH: Well – it was worth a try. Sorry to have taken up so much of your time, sir.

ROSS: (*Shaking hands*) That's all right. (*He looks at NASH*) I hope you'll break through that blank wall very soon.

NASH: Maybe we'll climb over it – and I've a feeling that when we do, we'll find something pretty unexpected on the other side. Goodbye, Mr Ross.

ROSS: Goodbye, Superintendent.

5

NASH goes out.

ROSS smiles after NASH, shakes his head and sits at the desk. He takes up the newspaper that NASH has left and looks at it for a moment, then, his mind turning once again to work, he places the newspaper aside. He takes up a file and opens it. In a matter of seconds, the "Bradford Case" is completely forgotten, and he is engrossed in the contents of the file.

A rap on the door and MAJOR LOCKWOOD enters. LOCKWOOD is in his late forties; a pleasant, military-looking man.

ROSS: Ah, Lockwood.

LOCKWOOD: Good morning, Mr Ross. I came in a few minutes ago but Hobson said you were engaged.

ROSS: Yes. Sorry to keep you waiting.

ROSS indicates a chair and LOCKWOOD sits. ROSS consults the file again.

ROSS: You don't know our Miss Thackeray, of course. You haven't been with us long enough.

LOCKWOOD: Miss Thackeray …

ROSS: She hasn't been in England for some years. She's working, ostensibly, as a school teacher in Hong Kong. (*He glances again at the file*) One of our best agents in the Far East. (*He looks at LOCKWOOD*) It's all right. Relax. I'm not sending you to Hong Kong.

LOCKWOOD: Well, I can't say I'm sorry to hear that.

ROSS: At least – not yet.

LOCKWOOD: Oh.

ROSS: Several weeks ago, Miss Thackeray sent me an interesting report. It was so

6

	interesting I thought we ought to get together and have a chat about it.
LOCKWOOD:	We?
ROSS:	Miss Thackeray and I. She arrives from Hong Kong tomorrow morning. As it's her first visit to England for some time I'd like you to meet her at the airport and take her to her hotel. I don't know what time the plane arrives. You'll have to check.
LOCKWOOD:	Yes, I'll do that, sir. Which hotel is it?
ROSS:	The Hyde Park. Get her report and tell her to phone me when she's settled in.
LOCKWOOD:	Very good, sir.

LOCKWOOD goes out. ROSS returns to his work on the desk.

CUT TO: London Airport. Day.
A jet plane is landing.

CUT TO: B.O.A.C. Arrivals Building at London Airport. Day.
LOCKWOOD is standing in front of the building, watching the passengers leaving the aircraft and walking towards the Arrivals Hall. The group – with the exception of three women and several children – consists entirely of men. Two of the women, and the children, are obviously in the same party. (Mother, Nursemaid, and children). The third woman is alone, she wears a light suit and carries a large handbag.

CUT TO: London Airport. Day.
The woman in the light suit is collecting her suitcase from a porter. LOCKWOOD stands in the background, watching her. His eyes travel down to the initials on her cases – "E.T." The woman is in her early thirties, good looking but

*distinctly tired after the journey. After a moment,
LOCKWOOD crosses to her.*

LOCKWOOD: Miss Thackeray?

The woman looks at him, obviously surprised.

THACKERAY: (*After a pause*) Yes?

LOCKWOOD: I'm Major Lockwood. Let me give you a
hand with those cases.

The woman hesitates, then smiles.

THACKERAY: Thank you.

CUT TO: Exterior of London Airport. Day.

*Outside the Airport, LOCKWOOD is just putting MISS
THACKERAY's suitcases into the boot of his car. MISS
THACKERAY is seated in the front of the car. LOCKWOOD
closes the boot, gets into the driving seat and drives off.*

CUT TO: In LOCKWOOD's car. Day.

*LOCKWOOD is driving. MISS THACKERAY opens her
handbag and takes out a packet of cigarettes. We see she is
wearing a thumb-stall. While she is engaged in this,
LOCKWOOD notices her perfume.*

THACKERAY: It was very kind of you to meet me.

LOCKWOOD: Not at all. It was a pleasure.

THACKERAY: Would you like a cigarette?

LOCKWOOD: No, thank you.

*MISS THACKERAY takes one herself, then fumbles in her
handbag for her lighter. She finds it and holding it in the
hand with the thumb-stall, has several attempts at lighting
it, but without success. LOCKWOOD glances at her and
sees the thumb-stall.*

LOCKWOOD: Oh. Let me …

THACKERAY: No. It's the lighter, actually. The wheel's
worn. I keep meaning to get a new one.

8

LOCKWOOD takes a box of matches from his pocket and gives them to MISS THACKERAY.

THACKERAY: Thank you.

MISS THACKERAY returns the lighter to her handbag and lights her cigarette with the matches.

THACKERAY: Thanks.

LOCKWOOD: Please keep them.

THACKERAY: Thank you. (*She puts the matches in her handbag*)

LOCKWOOD: What happened?

MISS THACKERAY looks at LOCKWOOD quizzically.

LOCKWOOD: Your thumb?

THACKERAY: Oh, it's nothing much. At least, I thought it wasn't at the time. An insect bite. Then yesterday it started swelling up.

LOCKWOOD: Have you seen a doctor?

THACKERAY: Yes – just before I left Hong Kong. He assured me it's nothing serious.

LOCKWOOD: Oh, good. Ross asked me to take you to your hotel.

THACKERAY: Thank you. It's very kind of you.

MISS THACKERAY smiles.

CUT TO: The Exterior of the Hyde Park Hotel. Day.

LOCKWOOD's car daws up outside the hotel. A Uniformed Commissionaire opens the car door.

CUT TO: In LOCKWOOD's car. Day.

LOCKWOOD: (*To the COMMISSIONAIRE*) There's two cases in the boot.

The Commissionaire salutes and moves to the boot of the car. MISS THACKERAY moves to get out of the car. As she puts her hand on the door, LOCKWOOD smilingly detains her.

LOCKWOOD: Miss Thackeray …
MISS THACKERAY looks at LOCKWOOD.
LOCKWOOD: The report …
THACKERAY: Report? …
LOCKWOOD: (*Smiling*) The tape …
THACKERAY: (*With a little laugh*) Oh, yes – of course.
             How stupid of me! I'm sorry …
MISS THACKERAY opens her handbag and takes out an envelope which contains a spool of recording tape. LOCKWOOD smiles at her and takes the envelope. MISS THACKERAY gets out of the car.

CUT TO: The Library, 29 Smith Square. Day.
ROSS is seated at his desk, reading a report. There is a knock on the door.
ROSS: Come in …
LOCKWOOD enters, wearing the street clothes he wore on meeting MISS THACKERAY at the Airport.
ROSS: … Lockwood.
LOCKWOOD: Good afternoon, sir.
ROSS: Well, did you meet Miss Thackeray?
LOCKWOOD: Yes. Everything went quite smoothly. I
             left her at her hotel.
ROSS: What d'you think of her?
LOCKWOOD: She was younger than I expected – and
             better looking. (*Smiling*) Wore a rather
             curious perfume. I've never come across
             one quite like it before.
ROSS: (*Smiling*) I didn't know I had a human
             bloodhound on my staff. I must remember
             that.
There is a rap on the door and EDWARD JONES enters. He is a senior civil servant in ROSS's department. He carries

*the tape which MISS THACKERAY handed to LOCKWOOD
in the car. He looks a little harassed.*

JONES: Excuse me, Mr Ross …

ROSS: Yes, Jones, what is it?

JONES: This tape from Miss Thackeray, sir … (*To
             LOCKWOOD*) You are sure this is the one
             she gave you, sir?

LOCKWOOD: Yes, of course I am.

ROSS: Why, Jones? What's the trouble?

JONES: Well, Mr Ross, as you know, I always
             decipher Miss Thackeray's reports …

ROSS: Yes …

JONES: But this one, sir …

ROSS: What about it?

JONES: I've just run it through, sir. It doesn't
             make sense.

ROSS: How d'you mean? She's using a different
             code?

JONES: No, Mr Ross. It's not a question of the
             code … (*To LOCKWOOD*) Are you sure
             this is the one she gave you, Major?

LOCKWOOD: I'm positive.

JONES: Then Miss Thackeray must have given
             you the wrong one.

ROSS moves around the desk to join JONES.

ROSS: How d'you know it's the wrong one? Is
             Miss Thackeray on it?

JONES: Yes, sir. But it's not a report, sir.

ROSS: Then what is it?

JONES: Just singing, sir.

LOCKWOOD: Singing?

ROSS: You mean it's Miss Thackeray singing?

JONES: Not exactly, sir. She's a schoolteacher out
             there in Hong Kong, isn't she, sir?

ROSS: Yes …

JONES: Oh well, that explains it, sir. Mr Richards
               said just now she was a schoolteacher –

ROSS: (*Impatiently*) What is on that tape, Jones?

JONES: Children singing, sir. With Miss
               Thackeray instructing them.

ROSS: In other words – a school singing lesson.

JONES: Yes, sir. And very nice it is, too.

*LOCKWOOD cannot resist a smile at this. But the smile
quickly vanishes as he sees ROSS's set expression.*

ROSS: It won't be 'very nice' if that other spool
               gets into the wrong hands.

*ROSS goes quickly to the telephone on his desk and lifts the
receiver.*

ROSS: (*On the phone*) Hello? Ross here … Get
               the Hyde Park Hotel and ask for Miss
               Thackeray …

*ROSS nods and replaces the receiver. He looks across at
JONES, then down at the tape in JONES's hands. He
indicates the tape recorder on the table.*

ROSS: Let's hear that.

JONES: This? Well, as I say, it's only – Yes.

*JONES goes to the tape recorder and puts on the tape.
LOCKWOOD, in the process of filling his pipe, joins
JONES at the recorder table. ROSS remains near the
telephone, awaiting MISS THACKERAY's call. He looks a
shade uneasy. JONES looks up, having finished putting the
tape on the recorder.*

JONES: Ready, sir?

*ROSS nods. JONES makes to start the recorder. The
telephone rings. ROSS takes up the receiver.*

ROSS: (*On the phone*) Hello? (*He listens for a
               moment with a puzzled expression*) Are
               you sure? … Who did you speak to? …

12

	All right. Thank you. (*He replaces the receiver and looks at LOCKWOOD*) Where did you leave Miss Thackeray this morning?
LOCKWOOD:	At the Hyde Park Hotel. Why?
ROSS:	Did you go into the hotel with her?
LOCKWOOD:	No. I simply dropped her at the door. Why? What's happened?
ROSS:	(*Quietly*) She never registered – there's no one at the hotel in the name of Thackeray. (*To JONES; quietly*) Let's hear that tape, Jones.
JONES:	Yes.

JONES switches on the recorder. They are all looking at it now. The recording, as JONES described, is of children singing, with a woman's voice interrupting them occasionally to offer advice and correct their faults. The song they are singing is an old Welsh folk song. They all listen in silence for a time. JONES smiles a little sadly as he listens; obviously the song has associations for him.

| JONES: | (*Almost inaudibly*) Well … |

ROSS looks at JONES.

ROSS:	You know it?
JONES:	Aye. But I haven't heard it for donkey's years.
LOCKWOOD:	It's a Welsh folk song, isn't it?
JONES:	Aye. Used to sing it when we were kids in the Rhondda Valley.

ROSS stares at JONES. JONES closes his eyes, softly humming in accord with the singing from the recorder. ROSS turns suddenly to the desk and takes up the telephone receiver.

| ROSS: | (*On the phone*) Hello? Get me Chief Superintendent Nash at Scotland Yard. |

CUT TO: The Library, 29 Smith Square. Day. The following morning.

The room is empty. The door opens and HOBSON shows in TIM FRAZER.

HOBSON: Mr Ross will be here in a moment, sir.

FRAZER: Thank you.

HOBSON goes. FRAZER takes a cigarette from his cigarette case and is just lighting it when MAJOR LOCKWOOD enters.

LOCKWOOD: Good morning. You must be Frazer.

FRAZER: That's right.

LOCKWOOD: I'm Lockwood. How-do-you-do?

FRAZER and LOCKWOOD shake hands.

LOCKWOOD: We have a mutual friend, I believe – Lewis Richards.

FRAZER: Oh, I see. You're – er –

LOCKWOOD: That's right. Another of Mr Ross's Merry Men.

FRAZER smiles. ROSS enters, he is brisk and business-like.

ROSS: Ah, I see you two have met.

FRAZER: Vaguely, yes …

ROSS: (*Crossing to his desk*) Well, take a good look at him, Frazer; you'll be seeing quite a lot of Lockwood in the near future.

FRAZER looks at ROSS, then across at LOCKWOOD.

ROSS: Yesterday morning an agent of ours, a Miss Thackeray, was due to arrive from Hong Kong. She'd recently sent me some important information and I wanted to discuss it with her.

FRAZER: Go on, sir.

ROSS: Lockwood went to the airport to meet Miss Thackeray. Unfortunately, the Miss Thackeray Lockwood met turned out to be an imposter.

FRAZER: (*Puzzled*) And the real Miss Thackeray?

ROSS: Two days ago, Superintendent Nash of Scotland Yard came to see me regarding the body of a Miss Bradford; she was found in a Pembrokeshire wood with her face battered in.

FRAZER: Miss Bradford?

ROSS: Yes – you've probably read about the affair. Melynfforest.

FRAZER: (*Thoughtfully*) That's right.

ROSS: Well, I've seen Superintendent Nash again and we're now convinced – quite convinced – that Miss Bradford was in fact our Miss Thackeray.

FRAZER: (*Puzzled*) But I don't quite … You say Miss Thackeray was supposed to arrive from Hong Kong yesterday?

ROSS nods.

FRAZER: And she was found murdered in Wales – let's see, when was it …?

ROSS: Two weeks ago.

FRAZER: But that's absurd! I mean – how did she get there? And what was she doing in Melynfforest, anyway?

ROSS: We don't know – and that's exactly what I want you to find out, Frazer.

FRAZER looks at ROSS, then at LOCKWOOD. He sits on the arm of the chair, facing ROSS.

FRAZER: All right. Go ahead. Let's have the rest of the story.

ROSS: The person who seems to have had most contact with the murdered woman was the local estate agent – a man called Roger Thornton. Miss Thackeray – Miss Bradford to the inhabitants, of course – was evidently looking for a cottage in the area.

FRAZER: I see. And where was she staying?

ROSS: At the St Bride's Guest House owned by a Mrs Crichton – where you will be staying for the next – (*Shrugs*) – for however long it takes to find out who murdered Miss Thackeray ... (*Pointedly*) And what she was after down there.

FRAZER: (*Nodding and turning to LOCKWOOD*) This other woman – the one you met at the airport yesterday ... What was she like?

LOCKWOOD: About thirty-three or four – good looking. (*Glances at ROSS*) She said she was Miss Thackeray – she had the right initials on her suitcases.

FRAZER: Anything else?

ROSS: (*A suggestion of sarcasm*) Lockwood noticed her perfume.

FRAZER looks at LOCKWOOD.

LOCKWOOD: It was rather exotic. Oh, and she was wearing a thumb-stall. Said she'd been bitten by an insect.

FRAZER: I see. (*To ROSS*) What was the point of this impersonation?

ROSS: We don't know. There appears to have been no point in the whole deception – apart from the tape she handed over.

LOCKWOOD:	The tape should have been her report, in code. It simply turned out to be a recording of some children singing.
ROSS:	Miss Thackeray worked as a school teacher in Hong Kong.
FRAZER:	I see. But is Miss Thackeray – the real Miss Thackeray – on the tape then?
ROSS:	Yes. (*To LOCKWOOD*) Play it for him, Lockwood.

LOCKWOOD goes to the table containing the tape recorder and switches on the recorder. The children singing the Welsh folk song are heard as before.

CUT TO: A Country Road. Day.
A small shooting brake is going along a road through hilly countryside, obviously Wales.

CUT TO: Guest House. Day.
The shooting brake comes along the road and it turns off into the entrance of the Guest House. The name St Bride's is seen over the entrance gates as the shooting brake goes up the drive towards the house.

CUT TO: FRAZER's Bedroom in the St Bride's Guest House.
A pleasant room, overlooking the garden. The furniture is of the heavy, solid variety. There is a wash basin in one corner. A telephone stands on a small table along with some copies of Country Life.
The bedroom door is open, and DAVY WILLIAMS enters, carrying two suitcases. He is fifty years old, porter, receptionist, and general handyman at St Bride's. He is at everyone's beck and call and looks always to the point of rebellion but, valuing his job, keeps his tongue to himself.

He grimaces as he listens to MRS CRICHTON's voice, talking to FRAZER as they come up the stairs. He has evidently heard this same old spiel many times before.

MRS CRICHTON: (*Off set*) Oh, I'm sure you'll love this part of the world. Practically everyone that stays here comes back again, you know. There are some glorious walks.

DAVY puts down the suitcases as MRS CRICHTON enters followed by FRAZER. MRS CRICHTON is a good-looking, well-educated woman in her early fifties.

MRS CRICHTON: Do you like walking, Mr Frazer?

FRAZER: Oh, yes.

MRS CRICHTON: The countryside's at its loveliest this time of year, I always think.

FRAZER: Yes. Yes, I agree. But I'm not here on holiday, you know.

MRS CRICHTON: Oh?

DAVY: Just the two cases was it, sir?

FRAZER: Yes. Thank you. (*He puts his hand in his pocket and gives DAVY some money*)

DAVY: (*With calculated surprise*) Oh, thank you, sir. Thank you very much.

DAVY nods and goes.

MRS CRICHTON: It's a very popular spot this, you know. In an exclusive sort of way, of course.

FRAZER: Well, I consider myself lucky that you had a room for me. You must be well booked up this time of year.

MRS CRICHTON: (*Carefully*) Yes. Yes, I am – as a rule, that is. But one does get those inexplicable periods when we're – not quite so full. Actually, it's one of those periods at the moment. That's why I was able to let you have this room. (*Anxious to change the subject, she moves to the window*) There's the view I was telling you about.

FRAZER joins MRS CRICHTON at the window.

FRAZER: Oh yes.

MRS CRICHTON: Most people find it quite breath-taking.

FRAZER: It is, indeed.

MRS CRICHTON: It's a little misty to-day. Heat-haze or whatever they call it. But on most days, you can see right over to Seaguard.

FRAZER nods. At this point music starts from a gramophone in the next room. It is a Beethoven Concerto. It is quite unobtrusive at the moment and FRAZER and MRS CRICHTON both appear oblivious of it as they look out of the window. MRS CRICHTON is naturally inquisitive about the nature of FRAZER's visit.

MRS CRICHTON: You're here on business then?

FRAZER: Yes. I'm with The British Research Corporation. They've asked me to make a report on the district.

MRS CRICHTON: (*Alarmed*) Oh, my goodness, I do hope that doesn't mean they're going to build factories down here.

FRAZER: Well, if they are, it won't be for yet awhile, I can assure you.

MRS CRICHTON: Oh, I do hope not. All this lovely countryside …

FRAZER: I shouldn't worry too much about it, Mrs Crichton. These things very often come to nothing. I wonder if you could help me, though. Do you know a local estate agent, by any chance?

MRS CRICHTON: Yes, there's one in the High Street. I think his name's Thornton. He's supposed to be very good.

FRAZER: Thornton …

MRS CRICHTON: That's right. Roger Thornton.

FRAZER: Thank you, Mrs Crichton.

The music has been getting louder while FRAZER and MRS CRICHTON have been talking and it now impinges on the conversation.

MRS CRICHTON: Oh – er – that music. I hope it won't bother you. It's Mr Elwyn Roberts – the gentleman in the next room. He's very fond of music. A retired gentleman. He's very nice but he will play his gramophone a little too loud at times. If it annoys you …

FRAZER: I'm sure it won't, Mrs Crichton. In any case, I shall be out most of the day.

MRS CRICHTON: Well – if it does, I hope you won't hesitate to let me know.

FRAZER: I won't.

MRS CRICHTON: And if there's anything else you require, please ask me.

FRAZER: Thank you, Mrs Crichton.

MRS CRICHTON smiles and goes. FRAZER looks after her for a moment, then takes up one of the suitcases and places it on the bed. The music stops.

FRAZER opens the suitcase and starts to take things from it, placing them on the bed. He goes to the chest of drawers and opens a drawer. The gramophone starts again. This time it is the Welsh folk song heard previously on the tape recorder in ROSS's office.

FRAZER is oblivious to the singing for a few moments. He takes some of his things from the bed and starts to place them in the drawer. He turns again to the bed and takes up a shirt. He stops as he turns to the drawers, suddenly becoming aware of the tune the choir is singing on the record. He remains there motionless for a moment or two, then turns to look in the direction of the room from which the music is coming. The singing continues.

END OF EPISODE ONE

EPISODE TWO

OPEN TO: FRAZER's Bedroom in the St Bride's Guest House.

FRAZER stands by the bed, shirt in hand, listening to the music. He goes to the door and out into the hall and moves towards ROBERTS's shut bedroom door. He stops by ROBERTS's door and walks back to his own room. He crosses to his bed and continues unpacking. He takes out his lighter. FRAZER examines it, takes his note book out of his case and goes to the telephone. He sits at the table and picks up the telephone receiver.

FRAZER: (*On the phone*) Would you get me Thornton's the Estate Agents please. It's Melynfforest 429 … I see … Ring me back when you've got a line will you? … Thank you.

FRAZER puts the phone down. There is a knock on the door. FRAZER crosses and opens the door. ELWYN ROBERTS is there.

ROBERTS: Sorry to trouble you – my name's Elwyn Roberts.

FRAZER: Elwyn Roberts?

ROBERTS: Yes, I'm the chap next door.

FRAZER: Oh, come in, Mr Roberts.

ROBERTS enters and FRAZER closes the door.

ROBERTS: I heard someone was coming into this room today, so I thought I'd better make sure about the old gramophone. I've had one or two complaints from Mrs Crichton. (*Smiling*) People saying I play it too loud.

FRAZER: Oh, it won't bother me, I assure you.

ROBERTS: Well, I thought I'd better make certain.

FRAZER: Thank you. My name's Frazer.

ROBERTS: (*Shaking hands*) How do you do, Mr Frazer? Have you stayed at Mrs Crichton's before?

FRAZER: No, it's the first time I've been to this part of the country.

ROBERTS: It's very pleasant – very pleasant indeed. You'll like it, I'm sure.

FRAZER: You're on holiday, I take it?

ROBERTS: Yes – permanently. (*Smiling*) I'm retired. I was a banker in Hong Kong.

FRAZER: Oh, I see. Have you been back there?

ROBERTS: Oh yes, many times. But what about you, Mr Frazer. What do you do for a living?

FRAZER: I'm with the British Research Corporation. I'm down here looking for building sites, that sort of thing. Probably come to nothing – but they pay my expenses.

ROBERTS: Sounds a fairly interesting job.

FRAZER: Yes, it's not bad. But I'm an engineer by profession.

ROBERTS: Oh, I see. (*He turns towards the door*) Well, I hope you like it down here. Nothing very exciting happens but … (*A thought*) Well, I don't know – perhaps I'm wrong about that ….

FRAZER: What do you mean?

ROBERTS: I was thinking of poor Miss Bradford – the murder. You must have read about it.

FRAZER: Miss Bradford? You mean the woman they found … (*Surprised*) Was that down here?

ROBERTS: Yes – right here, in Melynfforest. She was actually staying here, at Mrs Crichton's. Oh dear – perhaps I shouldn't have told you that.

FRAZER: Don't worry, if I know anything about this sort of place it won't be long before I hear the full story.

ROBERTS: I doubt it, Mr Frazer. I doubt it very much. No one seems to know the full story. Miss Bradford appears to have been something of a mystery … Still, I must admit, I got on pretty well with her. She'd travelled rather extensively so we had quite a bit in common …

FRAZER: Really.

ROBERTS: As a matter of fact, two days before she – died – she gave me a birthday present. Took me completely by surprise. Took a bit of explaining too, I'm afraid.

FRAZER: What do you mean – explaining?

ROBERTS: Well, I didn't know her very well, but naturally when the police started making enquiries, I had to tell them she'd given me a birthday present. It was all very embarrassing … But look, I'm talking too much – you want to get on with your unpacking. See you at dinner.

FRAZER smiles.

ROBERTS: Oh, if you want to hear some music, I've got stacks of records in my room. So just drop in and help yourself.

FRAZER: Thanks. I'll remember that. (*Suddenly: casually*) Oh – that record you played a little while ago … the children's choir singing …

ROBERTS: Which one was … Oh, the old Welsh folk song. Did you like it?

FRAZER: Yes, I did.

ROBERTS: (*Pleased*) It's a favourite of mine. I'll play it again for you some time.

27

ROBERTS nods at FRAZER then leaves. FRAZER looks at him for a moment and then goes over to the bed and examines his cigarette lighter. There is a knock on the door.

FRASER: Come in!

MRS CRICHTON enters.

MRS CRICHTON: Only me, Mr Frazer. I thought you might like to have one of these. (*She gives FRAZER a small booklet*) It's a local guide. Places of interest and a list of shopkeepers and so on. I think you'll find it very useful.

FRAZER: I'm sure I shall. Thank you.

MRS CRICHTON: By the way, I didn't give you the meal times. Breakfast is served between eight and ten – lunch at one o'clock and dinner at seven-thirty. Of course, we did arrange that in your case, lunch and dinner are optional. If you could just let me know each morning what meals you'll be wanting …

FRAZER: Of course. I'm sorry to be so much trouble.

MRS CRICHTON: No trouble at all, Mr Frazer.

MRS CRICHTON goes out. A few moments later there is another knock on the door.

FRAZER: Come in!

ROBERTS enters.

ROBERTS: Mr Frazer, I hope I'm not being a nuisance …

FRAZER: Not at all.

ROBERTS shows FRAZER a knife.

ROBERTS: But this was the birthday present I told you about. The one Miss Bradford gave me. I thought you might be interested.

FRAZER: Charming.

ROBERTS: Bit hideous, really, I suppose. Still, very kind
             of her to give it to me.

FRAZER looks very closely at the hilt.

FRAZER: What's this lettering on the hilt? Chinese?

ROBERTS: Yes. Would you like me to translate it for
             you?

FRAZER: Yes, if you can.

ROBERTS: It means (*He suddenly smiles*) "A present
             from Hong Kong."

FRAZER laughs and hands the knife back to ROBERTS.

ROBERTS: Thank you. Oh, by the way, I think I ought to
             warn you not to sit too near our Dr Vincent.
             Unless, of course, you're a keen golfer.

FRAZER: (*Smiling*) Hardly. I don't know a Birdie from
             a Bogey.

ROBERTS: Then I advise you to put at least three tables
             between yourself and poor old Vincent. He
             putts with the soup spoon and drives with the
             fish fork.

FRAZER laughs. The phone rings.

FRAZER: Excuse me.

*ROBERTS nods and goes out. FRAZER goes to the phone
and lifts the receiver.*

FRAZER: (*On the phone*) Hello, Mr Thornton ... My
             name's Frazer, I'm with the British Research
             Corporation ... (*A little laugh*) Yes, I expect
             you have ... Well, I'm taking a look at this
             area, Mr Thornton, and I thought you and I
             might get together ... Yes, if you've got the
             sort of thing we're looking for we'll be very
             interested ... Of course ... Right ... See you
             then ...

CUT TO: The Main Street, Melynfforest. Day
FRAZER's car drives along the street and pulls up outside the Estate Agent's office. FRAZER gets out of the car and crosses to look in the windows.

CUT TO: ROGER THORNTON's Office. Day.
The telephone is ringing. EVE TURNER lifts up the receiver. She is wearing a finger stall.

EVE: Roger Thornton ... Oh, yes ... I'm afraid he's very busy this afternoon, sir. Could you possibly make it tomorrow? ... Thank you so much. Goodbye.

EVE replaces the receiver and turns on her chair to face her desk. FRAZER knocks and enters.

EVE: Yes?
FRAZER: Good afternoon. I have an appointment to see Mr Thornton at three o'clock.
EVE: Mr Frazer?
FRAZER: That's right.
EVE: Mr Thornton's on the telephone. I shouldn't think he'll be long. Please sit down.
FRAZER: Thank you. (*He sits*)

EVE sits at her desk typing. FRAZER watches her. She stops typing and picks up her handbag, takes out her handkerchief, puts it on her desk. She takes out a cigarette and lighter. FRAZER rises and offers EVE a light.

EVE: Thank you.

ROGER THORNTON enters from an inner office.

THORNTON: Mr Frazer? Sorry to keep you waiting. How do you do?

THORNTON and FRAZER shake hands. They go into the inner office.

THORNTON: Turned colder this afternoon.
FRAZER: Yes, it has.

EVE inhales and sits back in her chair with a thoughtful expression.

CUT TO: The Inner Office. Day.
FRAZER sits in an armchair. THORNTON sits on the corner of his desk.

THORNTON: … Yes, I've heard of your organisation, of course, but I wouldn't have thought that they'd have been interested in Melynfforest.

FRAZER: That's what I thought. But you never know. They're prepared to buy sites if I can find them.

THORNTON: (*Thoughtfully*) M'm … Would make a tremendous difference to the place – a factory or two.

FRAZER: Only light-industry, of course.

THORNTON: Still … mean a lot of people coming to live in the area …

FRAZER: Naturally. (*Smiling*) And they'd all want houses to live in, Mr Thornton.

THORNTON: Yes … (*Also smiling*) I was thinking of that, Mr Frazer. (*He is obviously very pleased at the prospect. He takes out his cigarette case*) Cigarette?

FRAZER: I have one.

THORNTON: Is this your first trip to Melynfforest?

FRAZER: Yes. I'm staying at St Bride's.

THORNTON: Oh, Mrs Crichton's place. Do you like it?

FRAZER: Yes, I do. The food's very good.

THORNTON: Hasn't been doing too well just lately though, I'm afraid. You can probably guess why.

FRAZER: No, I'm afraid I … oh, you mean this murder business.

THORNTON: Yes. Extraordinary affair. I had several meetings with her, you know.

FRAZER: With Mrs Crichton?

THORNTON: No, no, with Miss Bradford, the murdered woman.

FRAZER: How did you meet her?

THORNTON: She was thinking of settling down here and I showed her several properties. The only place that interested her was Tregarn Cottage. (*An idea occurs to him*) Just a moment ... (*He goes over to a map of the district on the wall*) There's a piece of land just here which might be just the sort of thing you're looking for.

FRAZER joins THORNTON at the map.

THORNTON: Talking of Tregarn Cottage reminded me of it. (*Indicating on the map*) The cottage is just on the edge of the land here. The main road runs along here on the South side – which, as you know, is a great advantage in choosing a factory site.

FRAZER: Yes, indeed.

THORNTON: The land's not actually for sale at the moment, but the owner's definitely ready to sell if the price is right. I had a word with him several weeks ago when I was out there with – Miss Bradford.

FRAZER: Well – I might drive out there tomorrow. (*Looking at the map*) Let's see now, where are we ...

THORNTON: Melynfforest's not on this one. It's just to the West. That's the main road leading into it. Come into the outer office and I'll show you how to get there on the other map.

THORNTON opens the door.

FRAZER: Thank you.

CUT TO: The Outer Office. Day.

EVE TURNER is typing. THORNTON and FRAZER enter and go to the large map on the wall.

THORNTON: Here we are. Here's Melynfforest. There's Dawson's land there. That's the name of the owner.

FRAZER: I see. So I just stick to the main road all the way?

EVE rises and goes into the inner office. She leaves her handkerchief on her desk.

THORNTON: That's right. You can view the land from these other two roads bordering it, but they're pretty dodgy roads, I warn you. Specially this one leading down to Tregarn Cottage. There's a sharp bend here. Miss Bradford nearly came a cropper there one night when she was coming back from viewing the cottage.

FRAZER: Thanks for the warning. I'll take it easy.

THORNTON: Wait a minute. If you're going out that way, I've got a couple more places you might take a glance at. Small, but anyway, I'll get you the details.

THORNTON goes into the inner office. FRAZER sees the handkerchief on EVE's desk.

CUT TO: The Inner Office. Day.

THORNTON is at his desk getting some papers. EVE is at a filing cabinet. She returns to the outer office.

33

CUT TO: The Outer Office. Day.

EVE enters and sits at her desk. THORNTON hands FRAZER some property details and FRAZER prepares to leave.

FRAZER: Thanks, Mr Thornton, you've been most helpful.

THORNTON: Not at all. It's a pleasure.

FRAZER: Good afternoon, and thanks again.

THORNTON: Good afternoon, Mr Frazer.

FRAZER leaves. The telephone in the inner office rings.

THORNTON: It's all right, I'll take it.

THORNTON goes back into the inner office. EVE looks for her handkerchief but cannot find it.

CUT TO: A Bank by a stream. Day.

Fishing tackle, a basket etc are on the bank of a stream. LOCKWOOD, dressed in appropriate sports clothes is seated on the bank fishing. He sees someone approaching. It is FRAZER. They exchange greetings and FRAZER sits on the bank beside LOCKWOOD.

FRAZER: Any luck?

LOCKWOOD indicates the basket. FRAZER looks inside.

FRAZER: Two. Not bad.

LOCKWOOD: No.

FRAZER smiles.

LOCKWOOD: What about you? Have you managed to pull in anything yet?

FRAZER: Nothing very definite but staying in the next room to me is a retired banker who spends most of his time playing gramophone records.

LOCKWOOD: Well?

FRAZER: The day I arrived he was playing that song – the one we heard in Ross's office.

LOCKWOOD: (*Showing interest*) Have you met this character?

FRAZER: (*Nodding*) Name's Elwyn Roberts. Apparently, he became quite friendly with Miss Thackeray cum Bradford before she was murdered.

LOCKWOOD: I see.

FRAZER: They had something in common.

LOCKWOOD: Oh? What?

FRAZER: The Far East. Elwyn Roberts still spends a certain amount of time in Hong Kong.

LOCKWOOD: (*Nods*) What about this estate agent – Roger Thornton?

FRAZER: I went along to see him yesterday afternoon. He didn't seem to know very much about Miss Thackeray, except that she was very interested in a cottage. Tregarn Cottage. According to him she must have visited the place several times, presumably with a view to renting it.

LOCKWOOD: Have you had a look at this cottage?

FRAZER: No. Not yet. I'm supposed to be looking over some land Thornton's put me on to this afternoon.

LOCKWOOD: And to all intents and purposes Thornton's pretty genuine?

FRAZER: Thornton, yes. But he has a secretary … Lockwood, she's that woman who impersonated Miss Thackeray …

LOCKWOOD: Yes?

FRAZER: I seem to remember you saying something about the scent she was wearing.

LOCKWOOD: That's right.

FRAZER: Would you recognise it again; the scent I
               mean?
LOCKWOOD: Indeed, I would.

*FRAZER takes EVE TURNER's handkerchief from his
pocket and holds it to LOCKWOOD's nose. LOCKWOOD
inhales.*

LOCKWOOD: That's it. Thornton's secretary?
FRAZER: She's also wearing a finger stall.
LOCKWOOD: Then it's definitely the same woman.

FRAZER is taking two small photographs from his pocket.

FRAZER: Just to make sure … I took these.

FRAZER holds the photographs for LOCKWOOD to see.

LOCKWOOD: Rather more glamorous than she looked
               when I met her at the airport, but that's her
               all right.

*FRAZER puts the handkerchief and the photographs back in
his pocket.*

LOCKWOOD: What's her name?
FRAZER: Turner. Eve Turner. (*He looks at
               LOCKWOOD for a moment*) Look,
               Lockwood … Ross mentioned that Miss
               Thackeray was on to something pretty big.
               Now, I expect you'll tell me to get on with
               the job and mind my own business, but it
               would help me …

LOCKWOOD smiles and shakes his head.

LOCKWOOD: Relax, Frazer. I've had instructions to put
               you in the picture. (*Seriously*) Does the
               name Kurt Lander mean anything to you?
FRAZER: Kurt Lander? Yes, he's a German
               scientist. Disappeared just after the war.
               They were all after him. We, the
               Americans, the Russians, the lot …

LOCKWOOD: That's right. Well, a little while ago Ross received a report from Miss Thackeray. She was convinced that Lander was alive and was working in China. She told Ross that, in her opinion, there was a very good chance of getting him out of there.

FRAZER: I see. No wonder Ross was so anxious to meet Miss Thackeray.

LOCKWOOD: Exactly. But the point is, why on earth didn't she meet him – and what the devil was she doing in Wales under the name of Bradford?

FRAZER: (*Thoughtfully*) Yes …

LOCKWOOD: The police found a diary in Miss Thackeray's handbag. There was a note on today's date. "T.C. 4.15"

FRAZER: T.C. 4.15?

LOCKWOOD: In view of what you've told me, my bet is the T.C. stands for Tregarn Cottage and she had an appointment there with someone … I hope you find it a desirable residence.

FRAZER: 4.15?

LOCKWOOD: That's right.

CUT TO: The Exterior of St Bride's. Day.

It is late afternoon; about four-fifteen. FRAZER's car is parked on the drive just inside the gates to St Bride's. FRAZER comes out of the house and walks down to the car. He carries a mackintosh and is just putting this in the back of the car when DR NORMAN VINCENT comes out of the house. FRAZER closes the rear door and goes to the driving seat. DR VINCENT hurries over to him.

37

VINCENT: Mr Frazer – we haven't been introduced, I'm Dr Vincent – Norman Vincent.

FRAZER: How-d'you-do?

VINCENT: I hope you won't think it impertinent of me, but I wondered if you were going into town.

FRAZER: I am, yes. Can I drop you anywhere?

VINCENT: Well, I was just going up to the Golf Club to fix up a game for tomorrow. My car's in dock at the moment.

FRAZER: Jump in.

FRAZER leans into the car, unlocking the door on the other side.

VINCENT: Thank you.

DR VINCENT goes round to the other side and gets into the car. FRAZER gets into the driver's side. He starts the car and it sets off down the road.

CUT TO: Inside FRAZER's Car. Day.

FRAZER is driving. DR VINCENT is seated next to him.

VINCENT: It's only a mile or so, but I was afraid if I walked, I might miss the chap I want to see. Local chap. Only met him a few days ago. Incredible chap with a number three. What's your handicap, Mr Frazer?

FRAZER: I'm afraid I don't play golf.

VINCENT: (*Appalled*) You mean you've never played?

FRAZER: No, I'm afraid not.

VINCENT: Oh, my boy, you don't know what you're missing.

FRAZER cops the fact that the conversation is inevitably going to be 'Golf' all the way and decides to make the best of it.

FRAZER: Is it a good course down here?

VINCENT: About the best I've played on, I should say. My wife and I came here for our holidays every year without fail. She was a fine player – for a woman.

Silence for a moment. The "was" in VINCENT's last sentence is significant.

VINCENT: She was killed in a road accident five years ago. I thought I could never come here again. And then last year – I changed my mind.

FRAZER: You mean it happened down here?

VINCENT: Yes. Carreg Bend. A very dangerous corner about five or six miles the other side of Melynfforest. They need to do something about the place.

FRAZER: Yes. Someone mentioned it to me only yesterday. Said how dangerous it was. I'm sorry about your wife.

VINCENT: Yes, I've been a fool you know, staying away all this time. I have so many pleasant memories of Melynfforest. I'm in two minds about selling my place in Liverpool and settling down here. Are you just out for a drive?

FRAZER: No. I'm going to take a look at some land.

VINCENT: Where exactly?

FRAZER: Property that belongs to a Mr Dawson.

VINCENT: Oh yes, I know it. That dangerous spot I was telling you about – Carreg Bend –

FRAZER: Yes.

VINCENT: Well, it's on that road. For heavens sake be careful.

FRAZER: I will, I've already been warned about it.

VINCENT: Drop me here, Mr Frazer. The clubhouse is just on the left.

CUT TO: Country Road. Evening.

FRAZER's car is driving along the road. Carreg Bend comes into view. It is a sheer drop on one side down to a quarry. The car slows down to take the bend after which it carries on down the road. The road here has deteriorated into little more than a lane, with one open field on one side; a path across it leading to a cluster of trees. FRAZER's car slows down and stops. He gets out and walks to the edge of the path across the field. A small, roughly made signpost is stuck in the grass. It says on it: "Tregarn Cottage". FRAZER looks down at the signpost, then down the path. He starts to walk down the path.

CUT TO: Woodland. Evening.

FRAZER emerges from the trees. This is the other side of the cluster of trees we saw in the previous scene. He stops to look obliquely ahead. He can see Tregarn Cottage: it is attractive, yet isolated, nestling among the trees. FRAZER continues walking towards the cottage.

CUT TO: Tregarn Cottage. Evening.

FRAZER walks to both windows, looking in. It is obviously empty. He goes to the front door, taking a bunch of keys from his pocket. He tries several keys in the lock and eventually he is successful. He opens the door and enters. He pauses to glance around outside to make sure no one has seen his entry, and goes in, closing the door behind him.

CUT TO: Inside Tregarn Cottage.

FRAZER enters by the door of the cottage and slowly looks round. He comes forward and looks at the stairs. He goes into the centre of the room. EVE TURNER suddenly flings back the window curtains and steps forward. She is pointing a revolver at FRAZER.

FRAZER: Miss Turner. What are you doing here?

EVE: What's more to the point, Mr Frazer – what are you doing here?

FRAZER: I – I came out to inspect some land that Mr Thornton mentioned, and I thought perhaps …

EVE: Go on …

FRAZER: (*Looking at the revolver*) Well – I thought I'd take a look at this cottage …

EVE: I'm sorry. I don't believe you …

FRAZER: (*With a little laugh*) Well – you don't have to believe me …

EVE: It would be much better if I did, Mr Frazer.

FRAZER: What do you mean?

EVE: (*Tensely*) Who are you? Who are you working for?

FRAZER: I told Mr Thornton who I'm working for.

EVE: (*Interrupting FRAZER: angry*) Look, I'm going to give you five seconds. If you don't give me the information I want …

FRAZER: What information? I've told you …

EVE: Who are you? Who are you working for? What's your connection with Miss Thackeray?

FRAZER: Miss Thackeray? I've never heard of anyone called …

EVE: Five seconds, Mr Frazer!

FRAZER: (*Suddenly: making a decision*) All right. I'll tell you why I came to Melynfforest. I …

As FRAZER speaks the telephone rings.

EVE: Stay where you are, Mr Frazer.

EVE goes to the telephone and puts her hand on the receiver. As she does so FRAZER makes a move towards her. EVE whirls round and fires. FRAZER leaps over the sofa. EVE keeps firing the gun as she goes to the door and exits. FRAZER rises from behind the sofa. He sits on the arm of the sofa and bandages his hand with his handkerchief. The phone continues to ring. FRAZER rises to answer it.

FRAZER: (*On the phone*) Hello?

OPERATOR: (*On the other end of the phone*) Melynfforest two nine seven?

FRAZER: Yes ...

OPERATOR: I have a personal call from London – for Miss Thackeray.

FRAZER: (*Taken aback*) For whom?

OPERATOR: (*A little louder*) Miss Thackeray.

FRAZER hesitates, then:

FRAZER: Who's calling her?

Voices, indistinguishable are heard at the other end. FRAZER waits anxiously.

OPERATOR: Can Miss Thackeray take a personal call?

FRAZER: Who is it calling?

A few seconds of voices and then the operator is heard again.

OPERATOR: I'm sorry, but the party seems to have rung off.

FRAZER slowly replaces the receiver. He looks at his left hand: he pulls the bandage aside to enable him to look at his wristwatch. It says 4.30.

CUT TO: Country Road. Evening.
FRAZER's car is parked near the fields where he left it. FRAZER comes along the path from the cluster of trees. He reaches the car and gets into the driving seat.

CUT TO: Inside FRAZER's car. Evening.
FRAZER is in the driving seat. He is holding his left hand with his right, obviously in extreme pain now. He gives way for a few moments, his head leaning forward onto the

42

steering wheel. He pulls himself together and starts the car. He puts his left hand on the gear lever. He bites his lip as he makes an attempt to put the car into gear. He makes a second attempt, then realises it is useless. He hesitates for a moment, then gets out of the car.

CUT TO: Country Road. Evening.
A lorry is driving along the road heading for Melynfforest. The driver, EDDIE DAVIES, hums to himself as he drives. He stops humming, seeing something ahead. He changes gear, starting to slow down. FRAZER is in the road with his arms outstretched to halt the lorry. The lorry stops and FRAZER talks to the driver for a moment, then climbs up into the cabin. The lorry moves off.

CUT TO: Inside the Lorry Cabin. Evening.
EDDIE DAVIES is driving. FRAZER is seated at his side, nursing his left hand.
FRAZER: … Swinging my car and caught it on the bumper.
EDDIE: You look a bit rough. Here.
EDDIE takes a flask out of a cubby hole and hands it to FRAZER.
EDDIE: Whisky. Have a good swig.
FRAZER: Thanks.
FRAZER drinks and hands the flask back to EDDIE. EDDIE smiles and puts the flask back in the cubby hole.
EDDIE: How far d'you wanna go?
FRAZER: Melynfforest. I don't know where the hospital is
              but I think this hand'll need a couple of stitches.
EDDIE: I'll drop you there. Not far out o' my way.
FRAZER smiles gratefully.
EDDIE: Carreg Bend.
EDDIE indicates the road ahead with a nod.
EDDIE: 'Ell of a corner. 'Specially at night.

From inside the lorry cabin, we see Carreg Bend just ahead. As the lorry rounds the bend, we see a small car; it is up against the stump of a tree.

EDDIE: What the –

EDDIE applies the brakes sharply.

EDDIE: Look at this lot.

CUT TO: Carreg Bend. Evening.

A car is up against a tree stump. The driver has apparently taken the corner too quickly; the doors on the quarry side are open and it looks as if the occupants have been tossed out and are somewhere down the slopes of the quarry. The car is in such a position that it is obviously only the tree stump that has saved it from driving over the edge into the quarry. EDDIE's lorry stops and EDDIE and FRAZER get out and run towards the car. FRAZER reaches the car and looks inside. EDDIE's attention is arrested before reaching the car by something on the slopes of the quarry. He calls to FRAZER and starts to scramble down the bank. FRAZER comes around the car and sees what EDDIE is looking at; then he also scrambles down the slopes of the quarry. The camera pans to their objective – the body of a woman. They reach her.

CUT TO: The quarry on the side of Carreg Bend. Evening.

EDDIE and FRAZER are standing opposite one another, both looking down.   FRAZER evidently recognises the victim. The camera pans down to the body of the woman. Her clothes are torn and her face bruised, but she is unmistakably recognisable. It is EVE TURNER. She is lying partly on her back, her body turned slightly towards EDDIE. FRAZER crouches near the body and feels her pulse. He looks up at EDDIE and shakes his head. As he looks back at the body, he reacts to something.

EDDIE: Ruddy bend. That's the third crash this year.

FRAZER looks up at EDDIE.

FRAZER: D'you think so?

EDDIE looks perplexed. FRAZER indicates the body. EDDIE moves slowly round to where FRAZER is crouched. He stares down. FRAZER is looking up at EDDIE. For the first time we see there is a knife sticking in EVE TURNER's back. FRAZER looks at it. It is the knife ELWYN ROBERTS showed FRAZER at the guest house.

END OF EPISODE TWO

EPISODE THREE

OPEN TO: The Quarry at Carreg Bend. Evening.

FRAZER and EDDIE are staring down at the body of EVE TURNER. EDDIE DAVIES is standing, FRAZER crouched down by the body. We see the knife in EVE TURNER's back. FRAZER looks up at EDDIE.

EDDIE: You know her?

FRAZER: I've met her – yes. Her name's Turner. We'd better get the police. Where's the nearest telephone?

EDDIE: There's a box about half a mile on.

FRAZER: If you wouldn't mind …

EDDIE: O' course.

FRAZER: I'll hang on till they get here.

EDDIE: What about that 'and o' yours?

FRAZER: That can wait.

EDDIE: Right.

EDDIE remains there for a moment, staring at the knife in EVE's back, then starts to climb back up the quarry bank. FRAZER rises to his feet.

CUT TO: Carreg Bend. Evening.

The car is up against the tree stump. EDDIE comes up from the bank and crosses to the lorry. He gets into the lorry and drives off down the round. As the lorry departs, FRAZER comes up the bank towards the car. He goes to the open door side.

He sees nothing of interest and is just turning away when something underneath the car catches his eye. He bends down and takes up a handbag from between the front wheels of the car.

He opens the bag and empties the contents onto the bonnet of the car. There is a packet of cigarettes, a lighter, lipstick and powder compact, and a folded cablegram. FRAZER opens the cablegram, and we see what it says: It is

*addressed to EVE TURNER, 10 Bay Hotel, Hong Kong, and
was sent from Cardiff. It reads: "Will see you Kowloon 25ᵗʰ.
James." Frazer stares at the cablegram with interest and
curiosity.*

CUT TO: Carreg Bend. Evening.
*It is the scene of general activity. EDDIE's lorry has
returned to the scene. Several police cars and an ambulance
are also parked near the bend. Police are examining the car
against the tree stump and measuring distances etc. A
photographer takes a photograph of the group carrying the
body of EVE TURNER up the bank towards the waiting
ambulance. FRAZER and EDDIE stand by EDDIE's lorry.
DETECTIVE INSPECTOR ROYD is holding the knife, the
murder weapon, in a handkerchief.*

ROYD: (*To EDDIE*) Mr Davies …

*EDDIE is immediately apprehensive, although having
nothing to hide.*

ROYD: You can get along now if you want.

EDDIE: Well – I – er –

EDDIE looks at FRAZER, indicating his injured hand.

ROYD: That's all right. I'll run Mr Frazer into the
             hospital.

EDDIE: Oh. Right then …

ROYD: You gave your address to the Sergeant?

EDDIE: Yes.

ROYD nods. EDDIE smiles nervously at FRAZER.

EDDIE: Well – best o' luck, mate.

*EDDIE gets into his lorry. ROYD folds the handkerchief
around the murder weapon and puts it in his coat pocket. He
takes out his notebook. As he does so, the lorry starts up and
pulls away. ROYD consults his notebook.*

ROYD: Now, sir, your name is Tim Frazer and you're employed by The British Overseas Corporation?

FRAZER nods.

ROYD: According to Davies your car broke down a couple o' miles back …

FRAZER: That's right.

ROYD indicates FRAZER's hand.

ROYD: What happened?

FRAZER: Oh, I was trying to start my car and ripped it rather badly on the bumper. Davies was giving me a lift into the hospital.

ROYD: Davies said you knew the girl.

FRAZER: I said I met her once, that's all.

ROYD: Where?

FRAZER: In Roger Thornton's office. He's an estate agent in Melynfforest.

ROYD: When was this?

FRAZER: Yesterday afternoon.

ROYD: She worked there?

FRAZER: Yes. Her name's Eve Turner.

ROYD: Anything else?

FRAZER: No. As I say, I only met her that once – and very briefly.

ROYD nods and puts away his notebook. He takes out the murder weapon and slowly unfolds the handkerchief, revealing it. He studies it for a moment, then glances at FRAZER.

ROYD: You don't recognise this, I suppose.

FRAZER hesitates.

ROYD: You haven't seen it before, I mean? Not before today. Well?

FRAZER: As a matter of fact – yes, I have.

ROYD looks interested.

FRAZER: I'm staying at St Bride's Guest House. It was shown to me on the first day I arrived there.

ROYD: By whom?

FRAZER hesitates again.

ROYD: Well?

FRAZER: A guest. A man named Elwyn Roberts. He said it was given to him as a birthday present by Miss Bradford.

ROYD: Miss Bradford?

FRAZER: Just a few days before she was murdered.

ROYD: (*Thoughtfully*) I see.

ROYD starts to wrap up the knife once more. SERGEANT OWEN approaches. He is a plain-clothes SERGEANT and speaks with an obvious Welsh accent.

OWEN: We're all clear now, sir.

ROYD: Thank you, Sergeant. (*To FRAZER*) I'll run you into the hospital, sir.

FRAZER: Just into Melynfforest will be enough. There's a doctor at St Bride's. I should think he'd patch this up for me.

ROYD: Yes, I should think he would, sir.

ROYD walks towards his car. FRAZER starts to follow him, pulling the improvised bandage about his hand as he goes.

CUT TO: St Brides's Lounge. Evening.

It is late the same evening. The lounge is comfortably furnished with several armchairs, a settee, radio set, etc.

FRAZER and VINCENT are seated; VINCENT putting bandages, scissors and other things into a medical bag. He has just finished bandaging FRAZER's hand.

VINCENT: More comfortable?

FRAZER: Yes, thanks.

VINCENT: Good. Cigarette?

FRAZER: Oh, thank you.

VINCENT:	You were starting the car you say?
FRAZER:	That's right, yes.
VINCENT:	M'm … (*He muses for a moment*) You know, if you arrived at my surgery with a story like that, I just wouldn't believe you.
FRAZER:	No?
VINCENT:	No. I'd jump to the conclusion that there'd been a fight and that this was … (*Looks at FRAZER*) … a bullet graze.
FRAZER:	(*Smiling faintly*) You've too much imagination, Doctor.

MRS CRICHTON enters.

MRS CRICHTON:	Mr Frazer – Davy said you wanted to see me. I'm sorry I wasn't – (*She sees FRAZER's hand*) Oh. What's happened?
VINCENT:	(*Glancing at FRAZER*) Mr Frazer's had an accident starting his car.
MRS CRICHTON:	Oh dear. I'm so sorry.
FRAZER:	It's nothing very much. Dr Vincent's done a very good job on it. It'll soon be all right.
MRS CRICHTON:	Where did it happen?
FRAZER:	A mile or so the other side of Carreg Bend.
MRS CRICHTON:	Oh, dear! I hope you didn't drive all that way back on your own?
FRAZER:	No, I had a lift, Mrs Crichton. I've been looking for Mr Roberts but he's not in his room.
MRS CRICHTON:	No, I'm afraid he's out this evening; he's gone to a concert in Cardiff. (*She*

	looks at the clock) Although he should be back now. He said he was catching the nine o'clock train. Was it important?
FRAZER:	Well …
MRS CRICHTON:	(*Quickly*) It's not about his gramophone, is it? I do hope he hasn't been annoying you.
FRAZER:	No, no. I simply wanted to tell him not to go to bed just yet, that's all. I know he usually retires rather early, but I have an idea the police are probably calling round to see him.
MRS CRICHTON:	The police?
FRAZER:	Yes.
VINCENT:	(*To MRS CRICHTON*) This is very curious … Why should they want to question Roberts again? It rather looks as if some new evidence has turned up …
MRS CRICHTON:	Oh, why can't they leave us alone? We've told them all we know about Miss Bradford. (*Suddenly vehement*) Why did the wretched woman have to choose my house to stay in?

MRS CRICHTON turns quickly away from FRAZER and VINCENT. Immediately regretful of her outburst.

MRS CRICHTON:	I'm sorry. But what on earth do the police hope to find out by simply asking the same old questions over and over again?
FRAZER:	It's not about Miss Bradford this time, Mrs Crichton.

MRS CRICHTON and DR VINCENT both look at FRAZER.

FRAZER:	There's been another murder.
MRS CRICHTON:	What? (*Incredulously*) Another murder?
VINCENT:	God bless my soul! Who is it this time?
MRS CRICHTON:	Where did it happen, Mr Frazer?
FRAZER:	I'm afraid I can't say any more. The Inspector asked me ...

FRAZER breaks off on hearing voices in the hall.

DAVY:	(*Out of vision*) Into Cardiff, I think, Inspector.

FRAZER, VINCENT and MRS CRICHTON all look in the direction of the door. DAVY enters with INSPECTOR ROYD, who carries a small valise.

DAVY:	Inspector Royd to see you, Mrs Crichton.
ROYD:	Good evening.
MRS CRICHTON:	(*Nervously*) Good evening, Inspector.
DAVY:	It was tonight he was going in to Cardiff – Mr Roberts?
MRS CRICHTON:	Yes. Yes, that's right.
DAVY:	The Inspector wanted to have a word with him.
MRS CRICHTON:	Well – he should be back any minute now. Won't you sit down?
ROYD:	Thank you.

ROYD sits. DAVY looks on excitedly. MRS CRICHTON indicates that he leaves the room. DAVY scowls and goes. ROYD looks at FRAZER's hand.

ROYD:	How is it?
FRAZER:	Oh fine. Thanks to Dr Vincent.
MRS CRICHTON:	(*Blurting it out*) Inspector – I understand there's been another murder.

ROYD: (*Glancing at FRAZER*) Yes. Yes, I'm afraid there has. This evening. At Carreg Bend.

VINCENT looks at FRAZER and at his injured hand.

MRS CRICHTON: Who – who was it?

ROYD: A girl named Eve Turner. (*He looks at DR VINCENT and MRS CRICHTON*) Do either of you know her by any chance?

CRICHTON: Was she a local girl, Inspector?

ROYD: I'm not sure, Mrs Crichton, but she worked for a local firm, Thornton's, the estate agents.

MRS CRICHTON: Well, I might have seen her about. I suppose I must have done – but I certainly don't know her by name.

ROYD opens his valise and takes out the murder weapon. Both VINCENT and CRICHTON react to seeing the knife. ROYD looks at them as he holds out the knife.

ROYD: Have either of you seen this before?

MRS CRICHTON nods hesitantly.

VINCENT: Yes. Yes, we've both seen it.

ROYD: When?

VINCENT: Oh – several days ago. It – (*He hesitates and looks at MRS CRICHTON*) It belongs to Mr Roberts.

ROYD: Are you sure about that, sir?

VINCENT: It was a birthday present from Miss Bradford. Mr Roberts was rather fond of it, Inspector, he – made a point of showing it to us … one evening …

ROYD: (*Thoughtfully*) I see.

CRICHTON: Is that the knife that …

ROYD:	That killed Miss Turner? Yes, Mrs Crichton – this is the knife.
MRS CRICHTON:	Then Mr Roberts must have lied about going into Cardiff. He must have had an appointment with that poor girl and deliberately …
ROYD:	Now wait a minute, Mrs Crichton. I didn't say …
MRS CRICHTON:	You've got to arrest him, Inspector! You've got to take him away at once! He mustn't be allowed to stay in this house another day …
ROYD:	Mrs Crichton, wait a minute! Just because this knife belongs to Mr Roberts it doesn't …

Voices can be heard after the opening and closing of the front door.

VINCENT:	I think this is Roberts now …
ROYD:	Mrs Crichton, I don't want a scene while I question Mr Roberts. Perhaps if you would be kind enough to leave us alone together …

MRS CRICHTON glares at ROYD.

MRS CRICHTON:	This is my house, Inspector, and I shall please myself whether …

MRS CRICHTON stops as ROBERTS enters taking off his light mackintosh.

ROBERTS:	Evening all. Just started to rain. (*He hesitates as he sees the Inspector*) Oh. Good evening, Inspector.
ROYD:	Good evening, Mr Roberts.

MRS CRICHTON starts to walk towards the door. She changes her mind and goes to a small table on the pretext of tidying the magazines on it. ROBERTS puts his raincoat over a chair.

ROBERTS: Fancy. Never expected it tonight. Sky was clear as a bell when I left. Looks as though it's in for the night, too. That fine drizzle, you know.

As ROBERTS goes across to the others, ROYD slides the knife he is holding into his sleeve, his hand holding the end of it. This is unnoticed entirely by ROBERTS.

ROBERTS: Couldn't get a cab from the station. Had to walk. Well, Inspector, don't tell me you want to hear our stories all over again?

ROYD: No, Mr Roberts, I'm not concerned with the Miss Bradford case at the moment.

ROBERTS: (*Looks quizzically at ROYD*) Oh?

ROYD: Do you happen to know a Miss Turner. Miss Eve Turner?

ROBERTS: Eve Turner? Yes … Isn't she the girl who works for Thornton's the estate agents?

ROYD: That's right, sir.

ROBERTS: Thought so. Yes, I've met her, Inspector; she gave me some particulars of a property I was interested in … (*He stops. He is aware of the others watching him*) Why? What is it Inspector? Has anything happened to Miss Turner?

ROYD: She was murdered – this evening – at Carreg Bend.

ROBERTS: (*Appalled*) But – but – this is dreadful. How did it happen?

ROYD: She was stabbed in the back – apparently after a struggle with her assailant. Mr Frazer here found the body. At first, he thought it was an

accident. Her car was crashed up against a
tree.

*ROBERTS shakes his head. He is obviously shaken by the
news.*

ROBERTS: Dear me – this is terrible. Appalling! Do you
think there's any connection, Inspector?

ROYD: Connection, sir?

ROBERTS: Between this murder and the other one – Miss
Bradford's?

ROYD: Yes, I think there might be, sir. Two murders
in the same area – in the same month. It's a
bit too much of a coincidence.

ROBERTS: Yes. You say Eve Turner … was … stabbed,
Inspector?

ROYD: Yes. I've got the murder weapon here, as a
matter of fact.

*FRAZER and MRS CRICHTON's attention is riveted on
ROBERT's face as ROYD produces the knife. ROBERTS is
stunned on seeing the knife. He is speechless; makes no
comment.*

ROYD: Do you recognise it, sir?

ROBERTS: I recognise it … it … It's mine! It belongs to
me!

ROYD: When did you last see it, sir?

ROBERTS: Well, I … I don't know. Last night, I suppose.
It was in the drawer in my room …

ROYD: I understand it was a birthday present from
Miss Bradford.

ROBERTS: Yes … yes, that's right.

ROYD: You never told me about it, sir, when I
questioned you about Miss Bradford.

ROBERTS: I – I told you she'd given me a birthday
present.

ROYD: Yes – but you didn't say what it was.

59

ROBERTS: You didn't ask me.

ROYD: (*Quietly; after a moment*) That's quite right, I
             didn't. (*Suddenly*) And the last time you saw
             this knife was – last night, sir?

ROBERTS: As far as I can remember – yes.

ROBERTS becomes aware that all eyes are on him.

*He glances at MRS CRICHTON who is staring at him with
some kind of horrified fascination.*

ROYD: Can you account for your movements this
             evening, sir?

ROBERTS: Yes, of course. I've been to a concert in
             Cardiff.

ROYD: What train did you leave on?

ROBERTS: The four-ten. The one I always catch. It
             leaves me half an hour or so to eat some tea at
             the other end.

ROYD: And you left Cardiff Central at …

ROBERTS: Nine o'clock.

ROYD nods.

ROBERTS is becoming increasingly agitated.

ROYD: Have you anyone to verify these times?

ROBERTS: Verify …

ROYD: Did anyone go with you?

ROBERTS: No. I've been alone all the evening. I always
             am on these occasions …

ROYD: I see.

ROBERTS: I hope you're not doubting my word,
             Inspector?

ROYD: No, sir, but I wish you'd told me about the
             knife.

ROBERTS: But I did tell you – at least, I told you she'd
               given me a present. Oh, for heaven's sake,
               Inspector – it wasn't important … Any more
               than Dr Vincent taking Miss Bradford out to
               lunch was important – or her shopping
               expedition to Cardiff with Mrs Crichton.

*VINCENT and MRS CRICHTON look guiltily as ROYD
looks at them.*

ROBERTS looks uncomfortable.

ROBERTS: My feet are a little damp. Would you mind if
               I changed my shoes, Inspector?

ROYD: Of course not.

*ROBERTS glances in a half-heartedly apologetic way at
VINCENT and MRS CRICHTON and goes out taking his
raincoat.*

ROYD: Well, it seems Miss Bradford was a little
               more friendly than we thought. Still, it's Eve
               Turner I'm concerned with at the moment.

FRAZER: Inspector – what do you think happened
               exactly?

ROYD: I think Miss Turner had someone in the car
               with her. There was a quarrel and the car
               crashed. I think she jumped out of the car and
               … (*He looks at FRAZER*) the man followed
               her …

FRAZER: And who do you think this man was –
               someone she'd given a lift to?

ROYD: No, not necessarily – it may have been an
               acquaintance, or a friend of hers. He may
               even have been driving the car.

MRS CRICHTON: But the knife, Inspector … If Mr Roberts <u>was</u> in Cardiff this evening – then how –

VINCENT: It simply means that the murderer stole it from his room.

MRS CRICHTON looks aghast.

MRS CRICHTON: Then the murderer must be here – in this house.

MRS CRICHTON looks at FRAZER, then down at his hand.

ROYD: It's possible, Mrs Crichton. (*He looks at the hilt of the knife in his hand*) I wonder what the devil all this gibberish means?

FRAZER: Something very sinister, I'm afraid, Inspector.

ROYD: Oh?

FRAZER: A present from Hong Kong.

ROYD: (*Laughing*) A present from Hong Kong?

ROBERTS: Yes – and it wasn't the only one.

They all turn as ROBERTS has returned to the room.

ROYD: (*Seriously*) What d'you mean, sir?

ROBERTS: It looks as if Miss Bradford was pretty generous with her presents.

ROBERTS produces an identical knife.

ROBERTS: This is my knife.

ROBERTS glances round at the others.

ROBERTS: It was in the drawer in my bedroom. It's been there all the time, Inspector.

CUT TO: The Main Street, Melynfforest. Day.

A police car drives up to ROGER THORNTON's office. INSPECTOR ROYD gets out of the car, tells the driver to wait and goes into the office.

CUT TO: ROGER THORNTON's Outer Office. Day.

ROYD enters the outer office. He hears THORNTON give a cry of pain and goes in to the inner office.

CUT TO: ROGER THORNTON's Inner Office. Day.

THORNTON is on the floor surrounded by fallen files etc.

ROYD: Are you all right, sir?

THORNTON: Yes. Yes, thank you, Inspector. Just my shoulder. Stupid thing to do. (*He rises*) Reaching for a file from the top shelf. Lot of stuff on top of it and I thought I'd do it the easy way.

ROYD starts to pick up the fallen files.

THORNTON: Thank you. Don't bother with the rest. I'll pick them up later.

THORNTON goes behind his desk rubbing his shoulder.

THORNTON: Please sit down.

ROYD: Thank you. (*He sits*)

THORNTON: Well – this is a terrible business. I still don't believe it, you know. When you rang me this morning I was absolutely stunned. I was a little surprised when she didn't turn up this morning, of course. She'd never been late before …

ROYD: (*Nodding*) A good secretary, would you say?

THORNTON: Indeed, I would. The best one I've had.

ROYD: How long had Miss Turner been with you?

THORNTON: Let's see … (*He sits as he works it out*) October … five months.

ROYD: Where did she come from, do you know?

THORNTON: I don't – no. She showed me some references when she applied for the job, but I'm afraid I can't remember names.

63

ROYD: D'you know anything at all about her background?

THORNTON: No, I'm afraid I don't, Inspector, but she wasn't the chatty type – thank the Lord; I've had enough of those in the past.

ROYD: How did she come to work for you, sir?

THORNTON: My old secretary got married, I put an advertisement in the local paper and Miss Turner answered it.

ROYD: Mm … Was she a local girl?

THORNTON: Oh, no, – no. Definitely not. I think she was born in London, but I'm not sure.

ROYD: (*Nodding*) Can you tell me anything else about Miss Turner which you think might be of interest?

THORNTON thinks for a moment, then shakes his head.

THORNTON: No, I'm afraid I can't, Inspector. But perhaps her landlady, Mrs Elliot, can help you. I've got her address here …

ROYD: Don't bother. I've already seen Mrs Elliot.

THORNTON: Oh.

ROYD: I understand Miss Turner went to London fairly frequently?

THORNTON: Yes, she did. She only came back from there four days ago.

ROYD: And how long had she been in London?

THORNTON: On this occasion, three weeks. It should have been two, but her brother died while she was down there.

ROYD: Yes, Mrs Elliot told me. What about boyfriends, Mr Thornton?

THORNTON: Don't think she had any …

ROYD: Really? She was a very attractive girl by all accounts.

THORNTON: Yes, she was. She must have had boyfriends, I should think. She certainly never discussed them.

ROYD: Miss Turner didn't say where she was going when she left yesterday?

THORNTON: No, I'm afraid she didn't. She left here at her usual time.

ROYD: I see. (*He hesitates for a moment then rises*) Well, thank you very much, Mr Thornton.

THORNTON: Not at all, Inspector. Only wish I could be of more help. (*He rises*)

ROYD: Oh – I believe you're doing some business with a man named Frazer.

THORNTON: That's right. He's with the British Research Corporation. He's down here looking for possible factory sites.

ROYD: (*Nods*) Could bring quite a bit of business your way, eh?

THORNTON: If I can find what he's looking for – yes. (*Quizzically*) Did you – er – want to see Mr Frazer?

ROYD: No, I only mentioned him because it was Frazer who found Miss Turner's body.

THORNTON looks surprised.

ROYD: Well – thanks again. Sorry to take up so much of your time. (*He moves to the door. Stops*) Oh – just one thing. Where were you yesterday afternoon?

THORNTON: Me? (*After a slight hesitation*) I was in Seaguard on business.

ROYD: (*Nods*) Thank you, Mr Thornton. Good morning.

ROYD goes out. THORNTON sits in his chair rubbing his shoulder. It is obviously still quite painful.

65

CUT TO: St Bride's Lounge. Day.

ROBERTS is at the table reading a newspaper. FRAZER enters. ROBERTS looks up.

ROBERTS: Good morning. How's the hand?

FRAZER: Oh, much better this morning, thanks.

ROBERTS: Good.

ROBERTS indicates his newspaper which he folds up.

ROBERTS: Nothing in here about the murder.

FRAZER: Be in the evening edition, I expect.

ROBERTS: Yes. Quite a night out you had last night with one thing and another, eh?

FRAZER smiles faintly.

ROBERTS: Haven't long been up. All that business about the knife. Didn't get to sleep till gone three.

FRAZER: Yes, must have shaken you up a bit.

ROBERTS: Oh, it did. Tried not to show it, but it shook me all right. I was mighty relieved when I found my own knife, I can tell you that.

FRAZER: Mr Roberts, the other knife – the murder weapon – assuming Miss Bradford did give it as a present to someone, have you any idea who?

ROBERTS: (*Shaking his head in a vague manner*) No, I haven't the slightest idea.

FRAZER: Apart from yourself and Dr Vincent, who else was staying here with Miss Bradford?

ROBERTS: Oh, quite a few people. There's always someone coming and going you know.

FRAZER: Was there anyone in particular that she seemed to be friendly with?

ROBERTS: No, I don't think … Yes. Yes, now I come to think, there was someone.

FRAZER looks interested.

66

ROBERTS:	Not that she was particularly friendly. But she did talk to this chap quite a lot. At mealtime you see – they sat at the same table.
FRAZER:	Who was this man?
ROBERTS:	A fellow called Steinbeck – Carl Steinbeck. An American. Seemed quite a decent sort of chap …
FRAZER:	Have you any idea where he went to from here?
ROBERTS:	I understand he went up to London for a couple of days and then back to the States. The Inspector was obviously satisfied with him.
FRAZER:	What was he like, was he a typical American?
ROBERTS:	No, no, no, I wouldn't have called him typical not by any stretch of the imagination. Rather a nervous type, I should have said. Obviously a naturalised American.
FRAZER:	Naturalised? Why do you say that?
ROBERTS:	Well, he sounded like a German or Austrian to me. But Miss Bradford couldn't have given Steinbeck the knife, if that's what you're thinking.
FRAZER:	Why not?
ROBERTS:	Well – he'd have taken it back to the States with him.
FRAZER:	Unless he lost it – or it was stolen.
ROBERTS:	Yes. Yes. I hadn't thought of that.

DAVY enters.

| DAVY: | The man from the garage, Mr Frazer. |
| FRAZER: | Oh yes. Thanks, Davy. (*To ROBERTS*) My car. See you at dinner. |

FRAZER goes out.

CUT TO: St Bride's Drive. Day.

FRAZER's car is on the drive. A Mechanic is wiping the windscreen. FRAZER walks up to the car and greets the mechanic. He gets into the car and the mechanic watches him drive away.

CUT TO: The bank of a stream. Day.

A float of a fishing rod is bobbing about on the water. LOCKWOOD is sitting on the bank, fishing. FRAZER is seated beside him, holding the cablegram he took from EVE TURNER's handbag for LOCKWOOD to read.

LOCKWOOD: Was this in Eve Turner's handbag?

FRAZER: Yes. I found the bag under the car.

LOCKWOOD looks at the cablegram.

LOCKWOOD: (*Reading quietly to himself*) See you Kowloon, the twenty-fifth … James … Kowloon. That's on the mainland opposite Hong Kong.

FRAZER: Yes, so I gather.

LOCKWOOD: No specific rendezvous mentioned so it must be a regular meeting place.

FRAZER: Yes … looks like it.

LOCKWOOD: I'll get on to Ross and see if the name James means anything to him.

FRAZER puts the cablegram in his pocket.

LOCKWOOD: Apart from Miss Turner, did you find anything else at Tregarn Cottage?

FRAZER: No, not a … (*Stops abruptly*) The phone call.

LOCKWOOD: Mm?

FRAZER: So much happened after I left the cottage I almost forgot. The entry in Miss Thackeray's diary – T.C. 4.30. That referred to a phone call. There was a personal call for Miss Thackeray at 4.30. (*He looks at his hand*) It saved my life.

LOCKWOOD: A call for Miss Thackeray? Then the person calling couldn't have known she was dead.

FRAZER: Obviously not.

LOCKWOOD: That probably explains her visits to the cottage – she used the place for receiving phone calls. You know, Eve Turner must have known that call was coming through, Frazer, and was waiting for it.

FRAZER: Yes. That's my bet.

LOCKWOOD: Did you hear the voice at the other end?

FRAZER: Yes, it was a woman's voice, but very indistinct – talking to the operator. She rang off when she realised Miss Thackeray wasn't available.

LOCKWOOD: M'm. Well – anything else, Frazer?

FRAZER: Yes – Elwyn Roberts was telling me about an American called Steinbeck. He was at the guest house when Miss Thackeray was there.

LOCKWOOD: Steinbeck …

LOCKWOOD shrugs. Obviously, the name means nothing to him.

FRAZER: Roberts and I were discussing the knife that Eve Turner was stabbed with.

LOCKWOOD is studying FRAZER.

LOCKWOOD: I see. Well, don't get too involved in this Eve Turner affair. It's Miss Thackeray we're interested in. We want to know what she was doing in Wales – and why she was murdered, remember?

FRAZER: Yes, I know. I hadn't forgotten. (*Smiling*) I
                realise I haven't been sent down here on a
                fishing holiday.
LOCKWOOD: Seniority, Frazer, seniority.
FRAZER: I must be going. I want to catch Roger
                Thornton before he leaves his office.

CUT TO: ROGER THORNTON's Inner Office. Day.
*THORNTON is seated, waiting at his desk. FRED enters
from the outer office.*
FRED: Excuse me, Mr Thornton …
THORNTON: Yes?
FRED: Mr Frazer's here to see you. He hasn't got
                an appointment –
THORNTON: That's all right. Ask him in, will you,
                Fred?
*FRED goes out. THORNTON rises to greet FRAZER as he
enters.*
THORNTON: Ah, good afternoon, Mr Frazer.
FRAZER: Good afternoon.
THORNTON indicates a chair. FRAZER sits.
THORNTON: I gather from the Inspector you had quite a
                distressing experience last night?
FRAZER: Yes, I'm afraid I did.
THORNTON: (*Rubbing his shoulder*) Terrible business.
                You know, I still can't believe that it's
                happened. Been doing stupid things all
                day.
FRAZER: I know how you feel.
THORNTON: (*Sighs*) You read about these things in the
                papers but when it happens on your own
                doorstep … Completely bowled me over
                when the Inspector told me you'd found
                her.

70

FRAZER: Yes, it bowled me over too. I was on my way back from taking a look at that land you suggested.

THORNTON: Oh, yes. Dawson's. What d'you think of it?

FRAZER: Pretty fair. My people might be interested. Anyway, I've sent in a report.

THORNTON: Good. Before we go any further, I'd better get in touch with Dawson and make sure he wants to sell. Incidentally, after you left yesterday another proposition occurred to me. It's about half as big again as the Dawson site and only a mile and a half away from a new housing estate that's going up.

FRAZER appears to show great interest.

THORNTON: It's about six miles northwest of Melynfforest ...

THORNTON goes to the map on the wall.

THORNTON: Melynfforest isn't on this one, you remember, but the place I'm talking about is just –

THORNTON winces, clutching his shoulder, as he makes to raise his arm to point to the map.

THORNTON: Whee! (*He smiles apologetically*) I fell off a blasted chair this morning and pulled a muscle.

FRAZER: Have you seen a doctor?

THORNTON: No, but I will in the morning if it's no better. Anyway – look, I rang a friend of mine last night who lives on this new estate. He knows much more about the area than I do – number of unemployed and so on.

FRAZER: That's the sort of information we want.

THORNTON: I'll get the figures from him and drop them in to you. Friday morning be convenient?

FRAZER: Yes, that'll do fine. (*He crosses to the door, then hesitates*) I suppose the Inspector told you what happened – to Miss Turner, I mean?

THORNTON: Yes ... I ... I gather there was a struggle, and she was stabbed?

FRAZER: Yes, that's right.

THORNTON: Appalling business. Dreadful. A maniac, I should think. Probably the same person who murdered Miss Bradford.

FRAZER: Yes, could be. The poor girl must have given him a lift, I suppose.

THORNTON: I should think so.

The telephone rings.

THORNTON: Well, if you'll excuse me, Mr Frazer.

FRAZER: Yes, of course. I'll see myself out. You'll let me have those details.

THORNTON: I will indeed.

THORNTON goes to answer the phone as FRAZER goes to the outer office.

CUT TO: ROGER THORNTON's Outer Office. Day.

FRED: Good afternoon, sir.

FRAZER goes to the street door. He picks up his coat. He sees a poster and stops.

CUT TO: Cardiff Docks and surrounding area.

FRAZER walks into shot and stops to look at the Kowloon Hotel. Children are playing in the street. Coloured Seamen walk by. FRAZER crosses to the hotel, a Sikh comes out. FRAZER goes in.

CUT TO: Kowloon Hotel. Day

FRAZER enters and goes across to the bar and sits on a stool. STAN WHITE, who is behind the counter, watches him through the mirror over the counter.

FRAZER: Good morning.

WHITE turns to the counter.

WHITE: Yes? What do you want?

FRAZER: Tea, please.

FRAZER looks round the hotel. WHITE goes to the urn and pours tea and turns to FRAZER.

WHITE: Anything to eat?

FRAZER: No thanks.

WHITE: Just ashore?

FRAZER: No. I'm not a sailor.

WHITE: (*Sullenly*) Oh. Sugar?

FRAZER: Just one.

WHITE: You're not from this part of the world. Cardiff, I mean.

FRAZER: No.

WHITE, concealing his interest in FRAZER, fiddles with sandwiches etc on the counter.

FRAZER: I understand this place is for sale?

WHITE looks at FRAZER.

WHITE: That's right. Up for auction. Why? You interested?

FRAZER doesn't answer. He takes out his wallet, selects a five-pound note and places it on the counter.

FRAZER: I wonder if you can help me.

WHITE looks down at the note.

WHITE: Depends …

FRAZER: I'd like to get in touch with a man called James.

WHITE reacts to the name.

FRAZER: I'm told he comes in here now and again.

WHITE's attitude has changed suddenly. He is frightened.

73

WHITE: Who are you?

FRAZER: I don't think that matters …

WHITE: What's your name?

FRAZER: (*Slowly*) I'm a friend of Eve Turner's.

WHITE stares at FRAZER.

FRAZER: If you can get hold of James, I'd be very grateful.

FRAZER slides the fiver towards WHITE. WHITE stares down at it. He looks back at FRAZER, then turns and goes through the door into the kitchen. FRAZER looks after him.

CUT TO: The Kitchen. Day.

WHITE enters and goes to a wall mounted telephone. He lifts the receiver and dials a number.

CUT TO: Kowloon Hotel. Day.

FRAZER gets up and goes and locks the street door. He looks round and sits at the counter again. STAN WHITE returns from the kitchen.

WHITE: He'll be here in fifteen minutes. Oh, mustn't forget that, must we?

WHITE makes to pick up the five-pound note from the counter and in doing so knocks FRAZER's tea over.

WHITE: Oh, I'm sorry. Clumsy devil.

WHITE mops up the counter. FRAZER rises and brushes his suit.

WHITE: Not on your clothes, is it?

FRAZER: No. I'm all right.

WHITE: Good. Don't know what come over me. I'll get you another cup.

FRAZER watches WHITE through the mirror. WHITE takes another cup to the urn and after a moment pours out another cup of tea and turns back to FRAZER.

WHITE: There we are. Sorry about the other one.

FRAZER: Accidents will happen.

WHITE: Yes.

WHITE picks up the fiver and starts towards the kitchen door.

FRAZER: Oh – just a moment.

WHITE: Yes?

FRAZER: I'd like you to do me another favour.

WHITE: Well, what is it?

FRAZER pushes the cup of tea towards WHITE.

FRAZER: Drink this.

WHITE: What do you mean?

FRAZER: (*Producing a gun*) Drink it.

WHITE: Look here – who do you think …

FRAZER: (*Slipping the safety catch*) I don't think anything.
            Just drink it.

WHITE slowly lifts the cup and starts to drink the tea.

END OF EPISODE THREE

EPISODE FOUR

OPEN TO: Kowloon Hotel. Day.

FRAZER is seated at the bar levelling a gun at STAN WHITE.

FRAZER: Drink it.

WHITE looks down at the cup. He picks it up and slowly drinks the tea. He puts the cup down.

FRAZER: You'd better sit down.

WHITE goes to the counter and opens the flap. He comes round the counter and sits at a table. FRAZER rises from his stool and sits at the table.

FRAZER: This man James – who is he? What does he do?

WHITE: He owns this hotel.

WHITE bends forward over the table. FRAZER looks at his watch and at the door.

WHITE: I feel sleepy …

FRAZER: You'd better wake up. What else does he do?

WHITE: Huh?

FRAZER: James. What else does he do? What's his business?

WHITE: Business? This is – his business. This hotel. Kowloon …

FRAZER: You're not going to tell me this is the only thing …

WHITE's head goes down on the table. FRAZER shakes him. He then goes to the door and unbolts it. He looks back at WHITE then leaves.

CUT TO: A street in Tiger Bay. Day.

FRAZER is crossing the road coming from the direction of The Kowloon. He goes into a telephone booth and picks up the receiver.

CUT TO: The telephone booth. Day.

FRAZER is holding the receiver and making no attempt to put coins in the box or to dial. He is in fact using the booth as a vantage point from which to view The Kowloon. After a few moments he reacts to seeing something.

CUT TO: The street in Tiger Bay.

A Mercedes car is driven up to the hotel and a man gets out of it. He is LAURENCE JAMES. He looks up and down the street and goes in to The Kowloon. Fraser reacts.

CUT TO: The Kowloon Hotel. Day.

WHITE is still sprawled across the table. JAMES enters and stops dead on seeing him. JAMES is about forty-five, shrewd and ruthless. He goes to White, shaking him.

JAMES: Stan! Wake up! Wake up!

WHITE moans. JAMES looks in the direction of the counter. He goes quickly to the counter, takes up the teacup and looks back at WHITE. Guessing what has happened he slams down the cup angrily and goes back to WHITE. He grips WHITE's hair and pulls his head up.

JAMES: What's happened? (*He slaps WHITE*)

WHITE moans again. JAMES slaps his face. WHITE opens his eyes looking at JAMES stupidly.

JAMES: What happened?

WHITE: He … had a gun …

JAMES: Who did? Who was he?

WHITE: He must have seen me put the stuff in the tea because …

JAMES: Never mind about that now. Who was he?

WHITE: (*Shaking his head*) Never seen … never seen him before …

JAMES: (*Wildly impatient now*) What did he look like?

80

WHITE: Not the usual type. Not a sailor. Light suit –
           cream shirt – Had a plaster on his wrist.

WHITE begins to sag again. JAMES, with a disgusted expression, lets WHITE's head go, and it falls forward onto the table. He goes to the counter, taking up a bottle of soft drink and an opener. He opens the bottle, puts his thumb over the open neck, and goes back to WHITE. As he goes, he starts to shake the bottle in his hand.

JAMES: You dumb clot … What the hell do you think I
           pay you for? A piddling little job like that and
           you have to go and mess it up. Wake up!

WHITE doesn't sit up. JAMES grips his hair again, more viciously this time, and pulls WHITE's head up. He is still shaking the soft drink. He holds it horizontally near WHITE's face and releases his thumb from the neck of the bottle.

CUT TO: The Street in Tiger Bay.

FRAZER has left the telephone box and is nowhere to be seen.

The Mercedes is still parked outside The Kowloon. After a moment, JAMES comes out of The Kowloon, looks up and down the street, gets into the Mercedes and drives off.

CUT TO: Main thoroughfare in Cardiff.

JAMES's Mercedes comes along the road and stops at the traffic lights.

CUT TO: Inside JAMES's car.

JAMES looks idly around as he waits for the lights to change. FRAZER's car pulls alongside and halts at the lights. FRAZER has an unlit cigarette in his mouth. He glances at JAMES and takes out his cigarette lighter. He raises the cigarette lighter but delays the lighting of the cigarette. JAMES glances casually at FRAZER. As he does so, FRAZER lights his cigarette. JAMES looks away. FRAZER smiles faintly to himself. The traffic lights change and JAMES's car pulls away, leaving FRAZER's car behind.

CUT TO: INSPECTOR ROYD's Office. Day.
This is Melynfforest Police Station: the following morning.
ROYD is seated behind his desk, talking to DETECTIVE SERGEANT OWEN.

ROYD: No, the fact is … Frazer's story just doesn't tie up. He said he injured his hand when he was trying to start his car, and the mechanic at the garage swears there was nothing wrong with it. Where did the garage people find the car?

OWEN: Near Dawson's place – not far from Tregarn Cottage.

ROYD: That tallies with the spot where the lorry driver, Davies, picked him up.

OWEN: Yes. Davies said Frazer seemed genuinely shocked when they found Eve Turner's body.

ROYD: (*Dubiously*) That doesn't mean much, does it? Committing a murder, then going back and 'discovering' the body with a witness is a hell of a lot cleverer than suddenly disappearing.

OWEN nods.

OWEN: Yes, well – the fingerprints on the car may give us something to go on.

ROYD: Yes. Did you telephone Frazer?

OWEN: Yes, sir. He's on his way now as a matter of fact. I told him we wanted to take his fingerprints. Didn't appear to worry him.

ROYD nods.

OWEN: Incidentally, your favourite reporter's back in Melynfforest.

ROYD: What – Rita Colman? That's all I need.

OWEN: I saw her in the High Street this morning on my way in.

A knock on the door and a CONSTABLE enters. He looks flustered.

CONSTABLE: Excuse me, sir …

ROYD: Yes, Hughes, what is it?

CONSTABLE: The Chief Constable of the County, sir.

ROYD: (*Surprised*) What?

CONSTABLE: His car's just driven up …

ROYD: All right, Hughes.

The CONSTABLE nods and goes out. OWEN exits. ROYD quickly straightens his jacket, sees the full ashtray and empties it into the waste basket. He stands there a little apprehensively, awaiting the CHIEF CONSTABLE's entrance. OWEN enters showing in the CHIEF CONSTABLE, a pleasant, friendly man in his late fifties.

CHIEF CONSTABLE: Ah – good morning, Royd.

ROYD: Good morning, sir.

CHIEF CONSTABLE: (*To OWEN*) Thank you, Sergeant.

OWEN nods, glances quickly at ROYD, and goes out, closing the door.

ROYD: Quite a surprise, sir – seeing you here. Won't you sit down, sir?

CHIEF CONSTABLE: Thank you.

The CHIEF CONSTABLE sits. ROYD sits, looking at the CHIEF CONSTABLE with a faintly puzzled air.

CHIEF CONSTABLE: I've just received your report on the Turner case.

ROYD: Yes; I'm afraid we haven't come up with anything yet, sir. All we've got to go on at the moment are some fingerprints. We're checking them with the Bradford suspects.

CHIEF CONSTABLE: (*Hesitant*) Yes. Well – look, Royd – you mention a man called Frazer in your report.

ROYD: That's right, sir. He found the body. We're taking his prints this morning.

CHIEF CONSTABLE: He's staying at the St Bride's Guest House, I understand.

ROYD: Yes, sir. As a matter of fact, Sergeant Owen and I were just discussing Frazer. His story seemed to be sound enough at first, but in the light of further information … Well, I think he's definitely hiding something, sir.

CHIEF CONSTABLE: Yes … he possibly is.

ROYD looks interested.

ROYD: Do you know something about Frazer, sir?

CHIEF CONSTABLE: No, I don't. Not a thing. But he's the reason I'm here.

ROYD looks a little bewildered.

ROYD: I – er – don't quite understand?

CHIEF CONSTABLE: I've had instructions, Royd – from London. Rather odd instructions; but there you are. Whatever suspicions you may have about this chap Frazer – forget them. Furthermore, if he asks us for help at any time, we're to give it to him – and no questions asked.

ROYD makes to speak.

CHIEF CONSTABLE: And that includes me. So now you know as much as I do.

ROYD is speechless.

CHIEF CONSTABLE: Well, I'll be on my way.

ROYD: Yes ... (*He rises, not knowing quite what to say*)
          Well – nice to see you, sir.

The CHIEF CONSTABLE nods. ROYD moves quickly around the desk to open the door for him. He pauses before opening it.

ROYD: Frazer wouldn't be one of our own men, I suppose?

CHIEF CONSTABLE: (*Shaking his head*) No, and if it's any consolation to you, Royd – you're as wise as I am. Just don't question him as to his whereabouts and motivations, and give him any information that's available.

ROYD: Yes, sir.

CHIEF CONSTABLE: Well – goodbye, Royd.

ROYD: Good morning, sir.

The CHIEF CONSTABLE and ROYD shake hands then the CHIEF CONSTABLE goes out. ROYD closes the door behind him. He stands there for a moment with a bewildered expression. He wanders to his desk, and, abstractedly, lights a cigarette. OWEN enters.

OWEN: Frazer's here, sir.

ROYD looks at OWEN blankly. He evidently hasn't heard.

OWEN: Anything wrong, sir?

ROYD: (*A little irritatedly*) No, nothing at all. What did you say?

OWEN: Mr Frazer, sir. He's here.

ROYD reacts.

ROYD: (*Flatly*) All right. Wheel him in.

OWEN: We've taken his prints, sir.

OWEN is puzzled by ROYD's lack of interest.

OWEN: I said we've taken ...

ROYD: Yes, yes, I heard! You've got his prints. Well – now you can get rid of them; we don't want them.

OWEN: (*Blankly*) Yes, sir.

OWEN goes out and re-enters with FRAZER.

FRAZER: (*Cheerfully*) Ah – good morning.

ROYD: Good morning, Mr Frazer. (*Smiling*) Won't you sit down?

FRAZER: Thank you.

FRAZER sits. OWEN is surprised by ROYD's geniality towards FRAZER. ROYD gives him a look and OWEN goes out. ROYD proffers a cigarette box to FRAZER.

ROYD: Cigarette?

FRAZER: Thanks.

ROYD lights it for FRAZER.

ROYD: Well, Mr Fraser, I asked you along this morning to ask you a number of questions … (*He fingers his notepad*) … and to ask if we may take your fingerprints for elimination purposes.

FRAZER: Yes. They've just done that.

ROYD: I'm sorry. But they don't know yet whose they are, I mean. (*Smiling wryly*) Come to that, neither do I. (*Explaining*) The Chief Constable's just been here. He told me to drop any suspicions I had about you – and I might add they were pretty considerable – and to give you any information you require.

FRAZER smiles.

FRAZER: That's very generous of him.

ROYD looks at his notepad. He tears off the top sheet which obviously contains a list of questions he was going to ask FRAZER, screws it into a ball and throws it in the waste basket.

FRAZER: First of all, I'd like you to find out all you can about this character …

FRAZER takes out his wallet, extracts a photograph, and gives it to ROYD. ROYD looks at the photograph. It is

LAURENCE JAMES at the wheel of his car, turning to look into the camera. It is the photograph FRAZER took from his own car at the traffic lights. From ROYD's expression, the face in the photograph means nothing to him.

ROYD: Who is he?

FRAZER: A man called James. I think he must be pretty well known in the Tiger Bay area of Cardiff.

ROYD nods, still studying the photograph.

ROYD: James …

FRAZER: Doesn't mean anything to you?

FRAZER: No … I'm afraid it doesn't.

FRAZER: The number of his car's on the back, by the way.

ROYD: (*Looking at it*) 6457 ME – that's useful. Well – what do you want to know about him? The whole works, I suppose?

FRAZER: Yes, the lot. I think you'll find he fits in somewhere with Eve Turner.

ROYD: Eve Turner?

FRAZER: Yes – Eve Turner and Miss Bradford.

ROYD: You think the cases are connected, Mr Frazer?

FRAZER: Yes, I do. In fact I'm certain of it. There's one other thing, Inspector. As you know, I wasn't around at the time of the Bradford murder … but I understand there was a guest at St Bride's who left a few days after the murder. An American. Carl Steinbeck.

ROYD: That's right. As a matter of fact, he and Miss Bradford went out together several times. He was very upset when he heard about the murder. Quite genuinely, too, I believe. He had a concrete alibi, Mr Frazer.

FRAZER: Did he know Miss Bradford before she came to Melynfforest?

ROYD: No, I don't think so. They met at St Bride's.
           She arrived – let's see – two days after him, if I
           remember – that's right, two days.

FRAZER: You saw his passport ...

*ROYD smiles. This is an elementary detail he could not
overlook.*

ROYD: Yes, I saw his passport, Mr Frazer. He was an
           American citizen all right.

FRAZER: I understand he has a Central European accent.

ROYD: Yes, he had, but there's nothing unusual about
           that, sir.

OWEN enters.

OWEN: Excuse me, sir.

*OWEN places a note in front of ROYD. ROYD reads the
note and nods. With a glimpse at FRAZER, OWEN goes out.
ROYD picks up the note.*

ROYD: Mr Roberts has just telephoned – Mr Elwyn
           Roberts. You know that knife of his ...

FRAZER: The duplicate one?

ROYD: Yes, apparently, he's lost it – or at any rate, it's
           missing.

FRAZER: Missing?

ROYD: Yes.

FRAZER: And where is that one going to turn up, I
           wonder?

CUT TO: The Lounge at St Bride's. Day.

*ELWYN ROBERTS is seated in an armchair, looking at
DAVY WILLIAMS who is tidying the magazines and
emptying the ashtrays into a cardboard box on the table.
DAVY looks even more fed-up than usual.*

DAVY: I've already told you, sir. I didn't see it.
           Anyway, if it was in the drawer, how could I? I

don't make an 'abit o' going through people's things, sir …

ROBERTS: I wasn't suggesting that, Davy, I simply …

DAVY: Then why d'you keep askin' me if I seen it?

ROBERTS: (*Quietly*) I – I don't know why … I just thought I might have left it lying around.

DAVY: Look, sir – eight and a 'alf years I been workin' here and there's never been one complaint about my honesty –

DAVY breaks off, seeing FRAZER come in. FRAZER enters, having just returned from seeing INSPECTOR ROYD.

FRAZER: Good morning, Mr Roberts.

ROBERTS: (*Automatically*) Good morning.

FRAZER: Davy.

FRAZER smiles at DAVY who grunts a brief "Morning", picks up his box of cigarette ends and goes out.

FRAZER: What's the matter with Davy?

ROBERTS: I've upset him I'm afraid.

FRAZER: Oh.

FRAZER knows about the missing knife, of course, but cannot say so.

ROBERTS: My nerves are a bit on edge this morning – I – (*He breaks off with a sharp sigh*)

FRAZER: Anything wrong?

ROBERTS: Yes, there is … It's that knife – you know, the one Miss Bradford gave me. Someone's stolen it from my room.

FRAZER: Are you sure?

ROBERTS: Of course I'm sure! It couldn't just disappear, could it? I put it back in the drawer after showing it to the Inspector last night. When I went in the drawer this morning for my cuff links it had gone.

FRAZER: Are you sure you put it in the drawer?

89

ROBERTS: Yes, of course I did. In any case, I've
                  turned the whole room upside down!
                  (*He passes a hand over his brow*)
FRAZER: Don't worry, I'm sure it'll turn up.
ROBERTS looks at FRAZER.
FRAZER: In any case, it's no good getting
                  yourself worked up about it.
MRS CRICHTON enters with a key.
MRS CRICHTON: Ah, Mr Frazer, good morning.
FRAZER: Oh. Good morning, Mrs Crichton.
MRS CRICHTON: I saw you drive in. Your room key.
FRAZER: Oh, thank you.
MRS CRICHTON: Everything all right?
*MRS CRICHTON glances at ELWYN ROBERTS and one
feels that this is indirectly addressed to him.*
FRAZER: Yes, thanks. I'm happy to say I haven't
                  been so well looked after for years.
MRS CRICHTON: Well – I try to do the best I can for my
                  guests. Oh – have you just driven in
                  from the town?
FRAZER: Yes.
MRS CRICHTON: You didn't see Dr Vincent, I suppose?
FRAZER: No, I didn't.
MRS CRICHTON: Oh dear. I've had two telephone calls
                  from Liverpool for him and no one
                  seems to know where on earth he's got
                  to.
FRAZER: You've tried the Golf Club, I suppose?
MRS CRICHTON: First place I rang. But apparently he
                  hasn't been there this morning.
FRAZER: I may be going back into town after
                  lunch. If I see him, I'll let him know.
MRS CRICHTON: Thank you, Mr Frazer.
FRAZER nods and moves to the staircase.

MRS CRICHTON: Oh, Mr Frazer.

FRAZER stops. MRS CRICHTON moves to him, glancing back at ELWYN ROBERTS and speaking quietly to FRAZER.

MRS CRICHTON: I thought perhaps I ought to tell you – there's a young lady staying here for a couple of days. A Miss Colman – she's a journalist. She stayed here once before at the time of the Bradford affair. I thought I'd warn you, because she's bound to start asking you questions about Eve Turner.

FRAZER: Thanks for the tip, Mrs Crichton – but I daresay I can cope with a female newshound. (*Confidentially; smiling*) At the moment I'm having to cope with the police – which is far more difficult!

MRS CRICHTON: Yes – Yes, of course.

FRAZER smiles at MRS CRICHTON and goes out. MRS CRICHTON stares after him as he starts to go up the stairs.

CUT TO: Upstairs Landing at St Bride's. Day.

FRAZER reaches the top of the stairs, walks along the landing and puts his key in the hole in his door, opens the door and enters.

CUT TO: FRAZER's Bedroom at St. Bride's. Day.

FRAZER enters the bedroom and shuts the door. He turns and sees something on his bed. He walks towards the bed. There appears to be a body on it covered in a sheet.

FRAZER: Dr Vincent!

FRAZER pulls back the sheet to reveal a dummy body. It has a knife in it. The knife is attaching a message to the body. FRAZER is shocked and goes to the window and then goes back to the bed. He pulls out the knife and reads the message.

FRAZER: "It could have been you Mr Frazer".

DAVY: (*Out of vision*) Mr Roberts's knife.

FRAZER looks up and turns and sees DAVY standing in the doorway. He walks towards the bed.

FRAZER: Yes. It looks as if someone's got a strange sense of humour, Davy.

CUT TO: The Lounge at St Bride's.

ROBERTS: "Could have been you" … (*He looks at FRAZER*) Why *you*? I mean – you don't know anyone in Melynfforest, surely?

FRAZER: (*Wryly*) No, I'm afraid I don't.

ROBERTS: There must be a madman at large. It's the only possible … But how on earth did he get into your room? The door was locked, I suppose?

FRAZER: Yes.

ROBERTS: I don't understand it …

ROBERTS shakes his head and looks back at the note, then down at the knife which is in his lap.

ROBERTS: I wish to heaven that woman had never given me this thing …

FRAZER: May I give you a piece of advice, Mr Roberts?

ROBERTS: By all means – do.

FRAZER: Put the knife where no one can get hold of it. Either in the bank – or hand it over to the police.

ROBERTS: Yes, that's a good idea. A very good idea. I'll take it down to Inspector Royd.

FRAZER: Yes, I'd do that, Mr Roberts.

FRAZER nods and goes out. ROBERTS stares down at the knife in his lap. Tentatively, he takes it up, continuing to stare at it.

CUT TO: The Exterior of St Bride's. Day.
A taxi drives up to the front of the house and stops. DR VINCENT gets out, takes his golf clubs from inside the taxi and pays the driver. ELWYN ROBERTS, in outdoor clothes, comes out of the house and goes up to DR VINCENT. They exchange greetings. The camera pans in on them so we can hear the rest of their conversation.

VINCENT: Yes. I met some friends going down to Swansea for a round and went along with them. Two calls, eh?

ROBERTS: Yes. Mrs Crichton's been trying everywhere to get hold of you.

VINCENT: Oh. Shame. Well – see you at dinner.

ROBERTS nods. DR VINCENT swings his clubs over his shoulder and hurries into the house. ROBERTS turns to the taxi driver.

ROBERTS: Melynfforest Police Station, please.

ROBERTS gets into the taxi and it moves away.

CUT TO: FRAZER's Bedroom at St. Bride's. Evening.
FRAZER stands before the mirror, shaving with an electric razor. He examines his chin and, satisfied with it, switches off the razor and pulls the plug from its socket. He is just putting the razor in its case when there is a knock on the door. FRAZER looks up.

FRAZER: Come in.

The door opens and RITA COLMAN enters.

RITA: Excuse me dropping in like this – you are Mr Frazer, aren't you?

FRAZER: That's right.

RITA: My name's Rita Colman. I'm a journalist – from London …

FRAZER nods.

RITA: You've heard of me?

FRAZER: Not from your articles, I regret to say …

RITA: (*Smiling*) I know – from the police. I'm not very popular with Inspector Royd, I'm afraid.

FRAZER smiles.

RITA: Do you mind if I ask you a few questions, Mr Frazer?

FRAZER: Not at all – providing I don't have to answer them.

RITA: That's a charming beginning, I must say!

FRAZER looks at RITA for a moment.

FRAZER: (*Relenting*) All right – fire ahead.

RITA: Thank you.

FRAZER: You don't mind if I finish dressing while we talk?

RITA: Please do.

FRAZER takes up his tie and proceeds to put this on through the following:

RITA: Well, to start with, in case you're worried about hitting the headlines – I'm not a crime reporter. My paper's asked me to look into the Eve Turner affair because I happened to write a fairly successful article on Miss Bradford.

FRAZER: (*Casually*) Oh … You knew Miss Bradford then?

RITA: Yes – slightly. And I'm convinced that the two murders – Miss Bradford's and Eve Turner's – are in some way connected.

FRAZER: (*Lightly*) Yes, but that's pretty obvious, isn't it? I mean, a small town like this. Two murders are too much of a coincidence.

RITA: That's not what I'm talking about, Mr Frazer.

94

FRAZER: No? … Then what are you talking about, Miss Colman?

RITA: Eve Turner was stabbed to death and the knife was exactly like the one Miss Bradford gave to Elwyn Roberts.

FRAZER: Well?

RITA: Well – it's my bet that knife was also a present from Miss Bradford.

FRAZER: Now that's a very interesting theory. I should certainly have a word with the Inspector about that. Any other nice ideas, Miss Colman?

RITA: Yes – What about Tregarn Cottage?

FRAZER: (*Slightly surprised by the question*) Tregarn Cottage?

RITA: That's right. Don't tell me you haven't heard of Tregarn Cottage, Mr Frazer?

FRAZER: Yes, I've heard of it. Roger Thornton, the Estate Agent, mentioned it to me.

RITA: Miss Bradford was interested in that cottage.

FRAZER: Well?

RITA: The cottage was – or is – on Mr Thornton's books.

FRAZER: So?

RITA: Eve Turner worked for Roger Thornton. (*Smiling*) You see the connection, Mr Frazer? The knife – Eve Turner. Eve Turner – Roger Thornton. Roger Thornton – Tregarn Cottage. Tregarn Cottage – Miss Bradford.

FRAZER: Makes Tregarn Cottage sound like Clapham Junction. But I get the point. You know, you sound more like a detective than a reporter.

RITA: (*Laughing*) Just a simple journalist. But what about you, Mr Frazer? What are you doing in Melynfforest?

FRAZER: I'm with the British Research Corporation – and the only thing I'm investigating are the industrial possibilities of the area.

RITA: Fair enough …

FRAZER: But you've made me curious. Tell me about the other woman who was murdered – Miss Bradford. What was she like?

RITA: She seemed a fairly interesting woman. Her favourite topic was the Far East. She'd lived out there for quite a while.

FRAZER: Yes, so Elwyn Roberts told me. Were you actually down here at the time of the murder?

RITA: No; I'd just returned to London. When my paper found out that I'd met Miss Bradford, they sent me down to report on it.

FRAZER: Oh, I see. Now I understand. (*Smiling*) I couldn't quite see how you fitted in. While you were staying here – the first time – did you meet a man named Steinbeck, by any chance?

RITA: Steinbeck? Yes, I did. An American with a rather curious accent. (*She looks at FRAZER*) Why? What made you ask about Steinbeck?

FRAZER: (*Casually*) Oh, Elwyn Roberts mentioned him and it seemed strange to me that the police should let him go back to the States before they'd cleared the whole thing up.

RITA: Oh, he had a pretty good alibi. There was no question of keeping him here. But talking of Steinbeck – you've reminded me of something. I took a photograph of him and Miss Bradford, and unfortunately when I got back to London, I discovered that someone had tampered with the camera and exposed the film …

FRAZER: What made you take the photograph in the first place?

RITA: Oh, I'm always taking photographs, completely trigger happy when it comes to snaps. I took some awfully good ones of the Gower Coast last time I was down here. (*Reaching in her handbag*) I'll show them to you.

FRAZER: Isn't that rather forward of you?

RITA is interrupted by a knock on the door.

FRAZER: Excuse me.

FRAZER opens the door. DAVY WILLIAMS stands there.

DAVY: Excuse me, Mr Frazer, but …

DAVY stops, staring at RITA, then looks back a little disapprovingly at FRAZER.

FRAZER: Yes? What is it?

DAVY: Inspector Royd. He's downstairs. Wants a word with you.

FRAZER: Thanks. (*Getting his jacket*) Well – I'm afraid your questions will have to wait, Miss Colman – and the Gower Coast. (*To DAVY*) Showing me her snaps – makes a change from my etchings, doesn't it, Davy?

RITA smiles.

FRAZER: Excuse me.

FRAZER goes out. RITA goes to the door. DAVY is staring at her with obvious disapproval now.

RITA: (*Playing DAVY up*) I shouldn't let this get around. We don't want a guest house like this to get a reputation.

RITA goes. DAVY glares after her.

DAVY: (*Muttering*) Snaps, indeed.

CUT TO: The Lounge at St Bride's. Evening.

FRAZER enters and joins INSPECTOR ROYD.

FRAZER: Good evening, Inspector.

ROYD: Evening, Mr Frazer.

FRAZER: Davy said you want to see me.

ROYD: Yes – I – er –

ROYD glances at the open door. FRAZER goes to the door, closes it and returns to ROYD. ROYD continues.

ROYD: Your Mr James. I've got the information you wanted.

FRAZER gives ROYD an appreciative look.

FRAZER: Quick work.

ROYD: Well, we didn't have to look far for it. The Cardiff C.I.D. have had their eyes on him for some time, apparently – but they can't prove anything.

FRAZER: Oh – What do they suspect him of?

ROYD: They didn't say, Mr Frazer, but in the Tiger Bay area of Cardiff you can take your pick. He's a pretty wealthy man – big house in one of the suburbs; three cars. Owns quite a bit of property in the area.

FRAZER: Yes, I've seen some of it.

ROYD: (*Smiling*) Yes … calls himself an Export Merchant, travels about quite a bit.

FRAZER: Oh? Where?

ROYD: The continent. Occasionally the Far East.

FRAZER looks interested at this.

ROYD: Well – that's about it, I think.

FRAZER: Thanks.

ROYD: By the way, Mr Roberts called in on me this afternoon. Brought me that knife of his.

FRAZER: Oh, good.

ROYD: He said it was you that found it.

FRAZER: Yes, it was.

ROYD: Where?

FRAZER: In my room.

ROYD: But how on earth did it get there?

FRAZER: I haven't the faintest idea, Inspector, but whoever put it there is obviously anxious to get rid of me. There was a cosy little note to that effect.

ROYD: M'm – Well, watch your step, sir.

FRAZER: I will, Inspector. Oh, by the way, there's a friend of yours staying here at the moment – a Miss Colman.

ROYD: Oh, she's staying here again, is she? (*Gruffly*) Well – give her my regards. Good day, sir.

FRAZER: Goodbye, Inspector.

ROYD leaves. After a moment FRAZER turns to return to his room and finds DAVY in the doorway.

DAVY: Excuse me, sir. The laundry's arrived. Here's your shirts.

FRAZER: Thank you. I'll take them to my room.

FRAZER exits.

CUT TO: FRAZER's Bedroom at St. Bride's. Evening.

There is a knock on the door. FRAZER opens it and finds ELWYN ROBERTS outside.

ROBERTS: Mr Frazer …

FRAZER: Come in, Mr Roberts.

ROBERTS: Thank you. It was just that …

ROBERTS enters and FRAZER closes the door. ROBERTS stands listening.

ROBERTS: Ah, it's not as loud as I thought. Good!

FRAZER: Oh, your gramophone? No, that doesn't bother me.

ROBERTS: I'm so glad. I'd hate Mrs Crichton to receive any more complaints about it.

FRAZER: She won't receive any from me. Won't you sit down?

ROBERTS: Oh – thank you. (*He sits*) Inspector Royd was here, then?

FRAZER: Yes.

ROBERTS: Davy mentioned that he wanted to talk to you …

FRAZER: (*Noncommittally*) That's right.

ROBERTS: No more news, I suppose?

FRAZER: (*Shrugging*) No … The police don't give much away, do they? He simply wanted me to go over my story again. Incidentally, he told me about your knife. I'm glad you handed it over to him.

ROBERTS: Yes, it's a weight off my mind, I can tell you. I'm sure if I hadn't handed it in, something terrible would have happened.

FRAZER: Well, it's in safe keeping now, so you've got nothing more to worry about.

ROBERTS: M'm – one still can't get away from the fact that someone entered your room, and mine too for that matter. I don't trust anyone. Why, I even found myself suspecting … (*He hesitates*)

FRAZER: Suspecting me, Mr Roberts?

ROBERTS: Oh, good gracious, no! I wasn't referring to you, Mr Frazer! I know perfectly well you didn't have anything to do with it. Besides, you weren't even here at the time of Miss Bradford's murder – and everyone seems to think that both Miss Bradford and Eve Turner were killed by the same person. (*He shakes his head*) I'm beginning to wish that I hadn't

	been here ... Oh, dear – if only I'd remained in Hong Kong. (*He sighs*)
FRAZER:	That American you were telling me about, Mr Roberts – What was his name?
ROBERTS:	Steinbeck ...
FRAZER:	Yes – Steinbeck.
ROBERTS:	What about him?
FRAZER:	I just wondered what brought him to this part of the country, that's all. American tourists – you did say he was a tourist?
ROBERTS:	No, I didn't, but I suppose he was.
FRAZER:	Yes, well, American tourists usually confine themselves to London, Edinburgh and Stratford on Avon.
ROBERTS:	Yes, I know. I wondered about that too; but he said he'd been over here several times and thought he'd like to visit Wales for a change.
FRAZER:	I suppose if he wants to see Wales, Melynfforest's a good place to go.

The telephone starts to ring.

FRAZER:	Excuse me.
ROBERTS:	I'll be off, anyway. See you in the lounge later, perhaps.

ROBERTS exits. FRAZER answers the telephone.

FRAZER:	(*On the phone*) Tim Frazer speaking.

The muffled voice of the operator is heard saying "Go ahead, caller". A moment or two, then JAMES's voice is heard on the other end.

JAMES:	Hello? Mr Frazer?
FRAZER:	(*Faintly puzzled*) Yes ... Who is that?
JAMES:	My name is Laurence James.
FRAZER:	(*After a momentary hesitation*) Oh, yes. What can I do for you, Mr James?

We now start to cut back and forth between FRAZER in his bedroom and JAMES in a telephone box.

JAMES: Since you appear to be interested in me, Mr Frazer – I thought perhaps we might get together.

FRAZER: What makes you think I'm interested in you?

JAMES: You came down to my hotel in Tiger Bay – The Kowloon. You asked for me, didn't you?

FRAZER: Yes, I did. I was looking over various properties and saw yours was up for sale ...

JAMES: Mr Frazer?

FRAZER: Yes?

JAMES: I think I've got the property you're looking for.

FRAZER: (*A moment*) Then what would you suggest?

JAMES: I suggest we meet tomorrow morning at twelve o'clock.

FRAZER: Where?

JAMES: At The Kowloon.

FRAZER: All right – I'll be there. Twelve o'clock.

JAMES: (*Casually*) Oh, and before I forget ... Bring your overcoat, Mr Frazer.

FRAZER: (*Puzzled*) My overcoat?

JAMES: Yes, that's right. Your overcoat.

JAMES rings off. FRAZER remains there, receiver in hand, for a moment. He is obviously puzzled by JAMES's request. He replaces the receiver and goes to the wardrobe. He takes out his overcoat, looks at it, then goes through the pockets. He finds nothing in them. He shakes his head, puzzled. Music starts from the gramophone in the next room. FRAZER makes to put the overcoat back in the wardrobe. He stops, looking at it once more in an effort to try and find the answer to JAMES's request that he brings it with him. He stands there looking at the overcoat, utterly bewildered.

END OF EPISODE FOUR

EPISODE FIVE

OPEN TO: FRAZER's Bedroom at St. Bride's. Evening.
FRAZER stands at the table looking at his overcoat. He looks up. There is a knock at the door. FRAZER crosses and opens it to DR VINCENT.

VINCENT: Mr Frazer …

FRAZER: Oh, hello, doctor.

VINCENT: May I come in?

FRAZER: Of course.

VINCENT enters.

VINCENT: I was wondering how your hand was getting along?

FRAZER: Oh, it's fine now – thank you, Doctor. You made a very good job of it. I'll be able to take the plaster off tomorrow. Incidentally, I'm afraid I took your help for granted. You must let me know what your fee …

VINCENT: (*Interrupting FRAZER*) Nonsense, my dear fellow. Nonsense! Delighted to have been of service. Only make sure it doesn't happen again.

FRAZER: I'll do my best. I'm sorry I can't offer you a drink.

VINCENT: No, no, my dear fellow, that's all right. I'm T.T. anyway.

FRAZER: Dr Vincent, I'm glad you dropped in because there's something I wanted to ask you.

VINCENT: Yes, Mr Frazer?

FRAZER: When Miss Bradford was staying down here there was another man at the Guest House – an American called Steinbeck.

VINCENT: Yes, that's right.

FRAZER: I hope you don't mind my asking, but did you meet him?

VINCENT: Well – yes, in a casual sort of way.

FRAZER: What was he like?

VINCENT: (*Surprised*) What was he like?

FRAZER: Yes.

VINCENT: Oh – curious sort of chap. Not a bit like an American. At least not my idea of one. (*Amused*) Hated cigars, which is rather odd for an American to start with.

FRAZER: How do you know he hated cigars?

VINCENT: I offered him one. Told me in no uncertain terms what I could do with it. Odd sort of bird altogether. Pretty thick accent – Austrian or German, I should think. But why on earth are you interested in Steinbeck?

FRAZER: I'm with the British Research Corporation, as you know, and I've a hunch that Mr Steinbeck was working for one of our competitors.

VINCENT: Oh – you mean he wasn't really a tourist but was here on business? Getting the lay of the land as it were.

FRAZER: That's right. Quite a lot of the American companies are opening factories over here these days.

VINCENT: Yes, I suppose they are. (*Thoughtfully*) You could be right about Steinbeck, I suppose. I know he saw quite a bit of Roger Thornton, the estate agent, while he was down here.

FRAZER: Do you know Thornton?

VINCENT: Yes. Yes, we've played golf together once or twice. Nice chap. Incredible fellow on the green.

FRAZER: You say Steinbeck knew him?

VINCENT: Oh, yes – Steinbeck knew him all right. I saw them together several times.

FRAZER: Where?

VINCENT: Oh, in Melynfforest, and once I saw the pair of them in a car just outside Seaguard.

FRAZER: Were they alone?

VINCENT: No, there was another man with them. Thick set, rather a tough looking customer. (*Amused*) But, I say, you certainly are interested in our Mr Steinbeck!

FRAZER: I know these Americans. They're pretty tough competitors.

VINCENT: Yes, I suppose so. Although Steinbeck didn't look like a businessman, and he certainly didn't talk like one.

FRAZER: That was probably all part of the act.

The phone rings.

VINCENT: (*Puzzled*) Yes – could be.

FRAZER crosses to the phone.

FRAZER: Excuse me.

VINCENT: Yes, I'll be off anyway. Glad the hand's all right.

FRAZER: It's fine.

VINCENT goes. FRAZER answers the phone.

FRAZER: Tim Frazer speaking.

ROGER THORNTON's voice is heard on the other end of the phone. We don't see him.

THORNTON: Oh, good evening, Mr Frazer. Roger Thornton here.

FRAZER: Good evening, Mr Thornton. How's the shoulder?

THORNTON: Oh, not too bad, thanks. Still a bit stiff but nothing to worry about.

FRAZER: Good.

THORNTON: Look – that land I spoke to you about – this friend of mine called in today and gave me

109

	all the details. Unemployment figures, accommodation in the area, the lot.
FRAZER:	Oh, splendid.
THORNTON:	I can let you have them in the morning if you like. I have to drop in at your place to see Mrs Crichton.
FRAZER:	Oh, thank you very much. That'll save me a trip.
THORNTON:	Will ten o'clock be all right?
FRAZER:	Right.
THORNTON:	See you then. Goodbye.
FRAZER:	Goodbye. And thanks for ringing.

FRAZER replaces the receiver.

CUT TO: The Terrace at St Bride's. Day.

The following morning.

FRAZER's car is parked on the drive in the foreground. DR VINCENT is pacing up and down on the terrace. FRAZER comes out of the house. DR VINCENT turns.

VINCENT:	Ah, there you are, Frazer.
FRAZER:	Good morning, Doctor.
VINCENT:	Just waiting for a friend of mine to pick me up. Ought to get in a couple of rounds today.
FRAZER:	Weather's just right for it.
VINCENT:	I wanted to have a chat with you at breakfast, but you'd gone when I came down. (*In a confidential tone*) After I saw you last night I bumped into Davy. He told me about that business with Roberts's knife. The dummy and the warning note. What the devil's going on here?

110

FRAZER: Yes ... well, the knife's safely in the hands of the police, so I don't think there's anything to worry about.

VINCENT: M'm ... all the same, after two murders in the vicinity if I received a warning like that you wouldn't see me for dust.

FRAZER: (*Smiling wryly*) You wouldn't see me either if I were here for my health, but I'm here on business.

VINCENT: I don't know what to make of it. I don't really. Two murders and the police don't seem to have a single clue. Of course, they're looking for a madman, no doubt about that – no doubt at all. Trouble is, with these sort of fellows, you never know what's going to happen next. Well, I must be off. Probably see you at lunch. (*He goes*)

FRAZER: Hope it keeps fine for you.

FRAZER sits on a bench and starts to read a newspaper. A car arrives and footsteps are heard. FRAZER looks up. THORNTON joins him on the terrace.

THORNTON: Good morning.

FRAZER: Good morning. Lovely day.

THORNTON: Glorious, isn't it? Sorry I'm a bit late. Had a phone call just as I was leaving the office.

FRAZER: That's all right. I've nothing much to do this morning anyway.

THORNTON: Thanks.

THORNTON sits and opens his briefcase.

THORNTON: Well, I think this friend of mine's got all the information you need.

FRAZER: Good. It's very kind of you to take all this trouble ...

111

THORNTON: (*Smiling*) Not at all. (*He takes out a long envelope*) Part of my job. There we are. Some other odds and ends in there, too, about other available sites in the same area. Small, but you never know, you may have a buyer for them.

FRAZER: Thanks. I'm off to Cardiff this afternoon to take a look at a place.

THORNTON: (*A little surprised*) Cardiff?

FRAZER: Yes. The Tiger Bay area.

THORNTON: (*Doubtfully*) Tiger Bay … I wouldn't have thought there was much to interest you in that vicinity.

FRAZER: Perhaps not, but I thought I may as well have a look at the property.

THORNTON: What's the address? I know the area fairly well.

FRAZER: Oh, you know this one, I think. If I remember rightly, you've got a poster advertising it in your office. The Kowloon Hotel.

THORNTON: The Kowloon? (*He shakes his head disapprovingly*) Yes, it is on my books. Several other agents have been trying to sell it for months. May I ask who approached you about it?

FRAZER: A man called James. Laurence James.

THORNTON nods.

FRAZER: He owns the property.

THORNTON: Yes. That's right – and one or two other places in the same area.

FRAZER: Do you know him?

THORNTON: I've met him, yes. But I've never done any business with him. I've advertised his properties from time to time, but the places are falling to bits and the prices are ridiculously high. I haven't seen this Kowloon property myself, of course, but I can imagine what it's like.

FRAZER: (*Smiling*) Well – I promised James I'd take a look at it. I can make the most of it and stay overnight in Cardiff.

THORNTON: I expect Laurence James could help you there, too. He has a finger in almost everything in that area: entertainment for tired businessmen included, I should think.

FRAZER smiles.

THORNTON: (*Stands*) Well – Mrs Crichton's expecting me. I mustn't keep her waiting.

FRAZER: (*Stopping THORNTON*) Oh, Mr Thornton … Can you spare me a moment? Please sit down again.

THORNTON: Yes?

FRAZER: I was talking to Dr Vincent last night … (*Casually*) You've met Dr Vincent?

THORNTON: I have indeed.

FRAZER: He was telling me about a man who was staying down here a few weeks back – an American called Steinbeck.

THORNTON: Yes?

FRAZER: I understand you know Mr Steinbeck?

THORNTON: Did Dr Vincent tell you that?

FRAZER: Yes, he did.

THORNTON: (*Pleasantly*) Well, I should hate to contradict Dr Vincent.

FRAZER: Did you know Steinbeck?

THORNTON: (*Quite pleasantly*) Yes. But I fail to see what business it is of Dr Vincent's, or yours either, for that matter.

FRAZER: Well, I can't answer for Dr Vincent, but speaking for myself, I've got rather a curious nature, Mr Thornton.

THORNTON: And you're curious about Steinbeck?

FRAZER: Yes.

THORNTON: Why?

FRAZER: I'd like to know what exactly he was doing here, in Melynfforest.

THORNTON: He was on holiday; he was a tourist.

FRAZER: Is that what he told you?

THORNTON: (*Hesitantly*) Er – yes. (*Suddenly*) Look, I'll tell you what little I know about Steinbeck if you'll tell me why you're interested in him.

FRAZER: I have a hunch that Steinbeck was down here for the same reason as I am.

THORNTON: You mean – looking for suitable factory sites?

FRAZER: Yes. I think he was probably representing an American company.

THORNTON: (*Smiling: unable to conceal his relief*) Mr Frazer, you're dead right! Steinbeck was working with a New York property outfit, but he made me swear to keep the whole thing quiet. Whether it was a lot of hot air or not, I don't know, but he talked about buying heaven only knows how many acres all over the county. For about a week he had me really steamed up. I thought it was the jackpot.

114

FRAZER: Have you heard from him since he returned to the States?
THORNTON: I had one letter – but it was pretty evasive. I don't think you've anything to worry about, old man – competition wise. In fact, I'm sure you haven't.
FRAZER: Good.
THORNTON: (*Faintly patronising*) Still, it was pretty smart of you to get on to Steinbeck like that. I can see I shall have to watch you, old man, if we do business together. You're no fool.
FRAZER: (*Smiling*) I try not to be, Mr Thornton.

THORNTON goes into the house. FRAZER looks after him for a moment and then heads towards the drive. He gets into his car and drives off.

CUT TO: A Country Lane. Day.
LOCKWOOD is seated on a stile, smoking a cigarette. He hears a car approaching and jumps down from the stile, putting out his cigarette. FRAZER's car draws up. LOCKWOOD gets into the car, and it moves off down the lane.

CUT TO: Inside FRAZER's Car. Day.
LOCKWOOD is sitting next to FRAZER who is driving.
FRAZER: Sorry to bring you out in such a hurry.
LOCKWOOD: Not a bit. You sounded rather excited on the phone.
FRAZER: Yes. Things are moving pretty fast. We seem to be getting somewhere at last. I'm on my way into Cardiff to meet this chap James.
LOCKWOOD: I see. At his request?

FRAZER nods.

FRAZER: Yes, he rang me last night and suggested we get together to try and do a deal.

LOCKWOOD: What sort of a deal?

FRAZER: He said he has some property which my colleagues and I might be interested in.

LOCKWOOD: Do you think he's onto you?

FRAZER: Could be – after my first visit to The Kowloon.

LOCKWOOD: Why? What happened?

FRAZER: James's man behind the counter tried to slip me a Mickey and I slipped it back to him.

LOCKWOOD: (*Smiling*) Hardly suitable tactics for a representative of the British Research Corporation.

FRAZER: I wanted to talk to you before I met him because I thought you might have some ideas …

LOCKWOOD: Ideas? About what?

FRAZER: About a request he made on the telephone last night. It's got me stumped.

LOCKWOOD: Oh?

FRAZER glances at LOCKWOOD, then down at his own overcoat.

FRAZER: You've seen this overcoat of mine before, haven't you?

LOCKWOOD: Yes …

FRAZER: Do you notice anything peculiar about it?

LOCKWOOD: No, why? Haven't you paid for it?

FRAZER: I'm wearing it because James asked me to.

LOCKWOOD looks at FRAZER with a puzzled expression for a moment. He takes a closer look at FRAZER's overcoat.

LOCKWOOD: Bit of an odd request …

116

FRAZER:	It wasn't even a request really. When I agreed to meet him, he told me twice to bring my overcoat.
LOCKWOOD:	(*Thoughtfully*) M'm …
FRAZER:	I know the things you're thinking about. I've already been through them all. Secret document concealed in the coat collar – microfilm sewn into the lining!
LOCKWOOD:	(*Laughing*) Yes! But you've given it a good going over, I imagine?
FRAZER:	Every inch. There's nothing there.

LOCKWOOD is stumped.

LOCKWOOD:	What does this Laurence James do for a living?
FRAZER:	According to the Inspector, anything that brings in the loot.
LOCKWOOD:	I see.
FRAZER:	By the way – does the name Rita Colman mean anything to you?
LOCKWOOD:	Rita Colman? Yes, of course. She's a journalist. Wrote a couple of articles about the Thackeray murder.
FRAZER:	That's right. She stayed at St Brides at the same time as Miss Thackeray. She knew her as Miss Bradford, of course, same as the others.
LOCKWOOD:	But why the sudden interest in Rita Colman?
FRAZER:	She's staying at St Brides again, and last night she told me rather an interesting story about Steinbeck.
LOCKWOOD:	The American?
FRAZER:	Yes: apparently Miss Colman's camera happy and while she was down here, she

took a snap of Miss Thackeray and this chap Steinbeck.

LOCKWOOD: Well?

FRAZER: The film was never developed.

LOCKWOOD: Why?

FRAZER: Because when she got back to London, she found that the camera had been opened and the film was exposed.

LOCKWOOD: You mean – someone deliberately tampered with the camera?

FRAZER: That's right. The obvious 'someone' of course, being Steinbeck himself.

LOCKWOOD: In other words, Steinbeck was anxious that he shouldn't be associated with Miss Thackeray?

FRAZER: You're right, go to the top of the class.

LOCKWOOD ponders on this.

LOCKWOOD: Thank you. Doesn't tell us much though, does it?

FRAZER: No, not in itself. But I am sure it fits in this puzzle somewhere. And when we've solved it I think you'll find that 5 across and 6 down is Mr Laurence James.

LOCKWOOD: Yes – yes, I wouldn't be surprised.

FRAZER: On the other hand – he might be just a dealer in second-hand overcoats.

LOCKWOOD: Well, he won't get much for yours, will he? Drop me at this bus stop, will you?

FRAZER stops the car at the bus stop.

LOCKWOOD: Well – good luck. You might give me a ring when you get back. If he offers you more than fifty bob – take it!

LOCKWOOD gets out of the car and moves away from it. FRAZER drives off.

CUT TO: Outside the Kowloon Hotel. Day.
FRAZER's car drives up and stops outside the hotel.
FRAZER gets out of the car and closes the door. He looks at
the hotel. He walks up to the door and looks at a card
hanging on the inside of the glass panel. It says "Closed".
He remains there for a moment in a state of indecision.
Suddenly, the door is unbolted and opened. STAN WHITE
stands there. He looks at FRAZER with a faintly hostile
expression for a moment, then he stands aside and
grudgingly beckons FRAZER to come in. FRAZER enters
and STAN closes the door.

CUT TO: Inside the Kowloon Hotel. Day.
FRAZER enters followed by STAN WHITE.
FRAZER: Mr James not here yet?
WHITE: No. He rung a few minutes ago to say he'll be
              about an hour late.
FRAZER: An hour?
WHITE: He was called out on urgent business. Said to say
              he was sorry and thought you might have a bite
              to eat, or something till he gets here. Up to you.
              Paper there if you want it.
FRAZER looks round.
WHITE: Cup of coffee?
FRAZER: Thank you, but no.
FRAZER starts to take off his overcoat.
WHITE: Er – no hard feelings about the other day?
FRAZER: No. No hard feelings.
WHITE: Thanks. Mr James says I was to hang up your
              coat.
FRAZER hands his overcoat to WHITE who goes behind the
bar into the kitchen. There is the sound of a door closing.
FRAZER goes to the window and looks out. He sees a small
car has pulled up in front of the Kowloon. STAN WHITE

comes out of the side entrance and hands FRAZER's
overcoat to the car driver. WHITE returns into the bar and
the car drives off. FRAZER turns back looking thoughtful.
He looks at his watch.

CUT TO: A Room in a Warehouse. Day.
A man enters with FRAZER's overcoat. He hands it to
JAMES who is with a group of men. KURT LANDER puts
on FRAZER's overcoat. A photographer takes a flash
picture of LANDER in the overcoat.

CUT TO: Inside the Kowloon Hotel. Day.
WHITE and FRAZER are waiting by the bar. There is the
sound of a car drawing up outside.

CUT TO: Outside the Kowloon Hotel. Day.
A Mercedes pulls up outside the Kowloon Hotel. JAMES
gets out of it with FRAZER's overcoat and an envelope and
goes into the Kowloon.

CUT TO: Inside the Kowloon Hotel. Day.
JAMES enters carrying the overcoat and envelope. He nods
to WHITE to leave. WHITE goes into the kitchen.
JAMES: Mr Frazer?
FRAZER: Mr James?
JAMES: Yes.
FRAZER: Good afternoon, James. Or is it evening?
JAMES: Sorry I'm late. You got my message?
FRAZER: Yes.
JAMES: Your overcoat, Mr Frazer.
JAMES puts FRAZER's overcoat on a nearby chair.
FRAZER: Oh, thank you.
JAMES: Sorry Stan cut up a bit rough last time you were
          here. He didn't realise who you were.

120

FRAZER nods.

JAMES: He's not over-bright, our Stan. When you're dealing with his sort you have to spell it out in black and white who you're representing.

FRAZER: And you, of course, don't need the black and white treatment?

JAMES: (*Looking at FRAZER*) That's right ...

FRAZER: You know who I'm representing?

JAMES: That's right, Mr Frazer.

FRAZER: Well – what's your proposition?

JAMES: I've a very valuable property. I'm sure you'll be interested in it.

FRAZER: What do you call valuable?

JAMES: (*After a momentary hesitation*) Fifty thousand pounds ...

FRAZER looks at JAMES in silence for a moment.

FRAZER: That's valuable ... fifty thousand ...

JAMES: That's what I said ...

FRAZER: (*Smiling*) Do you seriously suggest that this hotel is worth ...

JAMES: (*Interrupting FRAZER*) I'm not talking about this hotel. You know what I'm talking about.

FRAZER: Don't over-estimate me, Mr James. I'm not at all sure that I know what you're talking about.

JAMES: (*Leaning towards FRAZER*) Look – I've got Kurt Lander and I want fifty thousand pounds for him.

There is a pause.

FRAZER: How do I know that you've got Lander?

JAMES looks at FRAZER for a moment, then opens the envelope he brought in with him and takes out a photograph. He smiles at FRAZER, then hands him the photograph. FRAZER looks at the photograph. He gives no sign of recognition of the man in the photograph.

JAMES:	Well?
FRAZER:	When was this taken?
JAMES:	Less than an hour ago.
FRAZER:	How do I know that?
JAMES:	(*Smiling*) He's wearing your overcoat, Mr Frazer.

FRAZER looks at the photograph and puts it on the bar.

CUT TO: The Library, 29 Smith Square, London. Day.
CHARLES ROSS is holding the photograph of KURT LANDER wearing FRAZER's overcoat. He walks to his desk and picks up another photograph from the desk and compares them. LOCKWOOD and FRAZER are seated on the other side of the desk.

ROSS:	Yes, it's Kurt Lander all right.
FRAZER:	I showed Inspector Royd the photograph; he identified the man as Steinbeck.
LOCKWOOD:	You mean – Lander and Steinbeck are the same person?
FRAZER:	Yes.
LOCKWOOD:	(*To ROSS*) Do you think Miss Thackeray knew that, sir?
ROSS:	Yes, I do. That report she sent said she had a plan for getting Lander out of China. She must have put it into operation then let Lander slip through her fingers.
LOCKWOOD:	Yes, it's the old story – someone obviously persuaded Lander to double-cross the very people who had helped him to escape.
FRAZER:	That doesn't sound very possible …
ROSS:	Maybe not, but it's been done before, Frazer. You'd be surprised. Conflicting loyalties are something we're used to in

this department. (*To LOCKWOOD*) Miss Thackeray obviously followed Lander to Wales and was trying to get him to come over to us when she was murdered.

FRAZER: But why didn't she get in touch with us instead of trying to pull it off on her own?

ROSS: If you'd ever met Miss Thackeray, you wouldn't ask that question, Frazer. She was a lone operator: half the time even I didn't know what she was up to myself.

ROSS picks up the photograph again and looks at it.

ROSS: No, the thing that worried me about this business is the photograph.

FRAZER: The photograph?

ROSS: Yes. The camera is the biggest liar of all time. This photograph could be faked. It might even be an old one of Lander.

FRAZER: No, sir. I don't agree. That's my overcoat all right.

ROSS looks at FRAZER.

FRAZER: They went to a great deal of trouble to borrow my overcoat. They photographed Lander in it and gave me that picture – all within the space of an hour.

LOCKWOOD: I agree with Frazer, sir.

ROSS: You think they've got Lander?

LOCKWOOD: I do. I do, indeed.

FRAZER: They've got him all right, sir – I don't think there's any doubt about that.

ROSS: M'm. (*To FRAZER*) Well, in that case, do you think this man James knows your real identity?

FRAZER: No, I don't think so; although obviously he knows I'm not working for the British

	Research Corporation. Curiously enough I've got the feeling … (*He hesitates*)
ROSS:	Go on …
FRAZER:	Well, I've got the feeling he's mistaken me for someone else.
ROSS:	You mean – someone he's been expecting? A stranger – but a contact?
FRAZER:	Yes.
ROSS:	(*Nodding*) That makes sense to me.
LOCKWOOD:	In which case, the person he's been waiting for might still turn up.
FRAZER:	Yes.
ROSS:	(*Suddenly: a decision*) Frazer, go ahead. Get in touch with James. Do a deal with him.
FRAZER:	(*Smiling*) And what do I use for money?
ROSS:	Money is the least of our problems. (*He looks at FRAZER and smiles*) We'll pay fifty thousand for Lander – more if necessary. He's one of the few men who really knows what the scientists are up to in Red China.
FRAZER:	Yes, but the trouble is, I don't know Lander – apart from the photographs. And obviously I've got to see him, before we hand the money over.
ROSS:	We've got a file on him. I'll see you're fully briefed before you leave. Now – you say they took this photograph, developed it, and got it back to you within the hour?
FRAZER:	Yes.
ROSS:	And you were in Cardiff?
FRAZER:	Yes, at The Kowloon.

ROSS looks musingly down at the photograph.

ROSS: Then – Lander couldn't have been very far away
           …

CUT TO: Inside the Kowloon Hotel. Day.
*STAN WHITE is behind the bar pouring a drink. TUG
WALLIS is seated on a stool at the bar. STAN finishes
pouring the drink and raises it to someone out of shot.*
WHITE: All the best, Miss.
*We see RITA seated at the bar further along from TUG
WALLIS.*
RITA: Skoal!
STAN WHITE drinks, then grins at RITA.
RITA: Not very busy today?
WHITE: Comes and goes, you know.
RITA: Are you the boss?
WHITE: No, no. Not me. This place belongs to a chap
          called James.
RITA: James … I seem to have heard the name.
WHITE gives TUG WALLIS a glance.
WHITE: Not many that haven't round these parts.
RITA: Really? Then it sounds as if Mr James and I
          ought to get acquainted.
WHITE: Oh?
RITA: I'm a journalist. I'm writing a few articles about
          Tiger Bay and the people who live down here.
TUG: Oh – well, if you'll excuse me, Miss, you want
          to try that new coffee bar further down the road.
WHITE: (*Disgustedly*) Ach! Coffee Bars!
TUG: That's where they all go, Stan – these writers
          lookin' for summat to write about. They all go to
          the coffee bars.
WHITE: What's the matter with writin' about this place?
          We get all sorts 'ere.
TUG: I don't see much sign of 'em.

WHITE: They'll be in.

RITA gets off the stool and finishes her drink.

RITA: All right. I'll look in later. (*To TUG*) Where is this coffee bar?

TUG: Just under the railway bridge. Turn left as you go out.

RITA: Thanks. See you later.

RITA leaves.

TUG: (*To WHITE*) What the 'ell's the matter with you?

WHITE: What do you mean?

TUG: Telling her to stick around when I was doing my best to get rid of 'er. Nosey tarts! We don't want the likes of 'er hanging around. What's James going to say? Where is he, anyhow?

WHITE: Should be here any minute.

The sound of a car driving up outside is heard.

WHITE: Sounds like him now.

TUG: About time, too. Let's see a bit of action around 'ere.

JAMES comes in. He nods to TUG and then looks at WHITE.

JAMES: Has he arrived?

WHITE: (*Blankly*) Who?

JAMES: For heaven's sake, Stan – you know who I mean!

WHITE: Oh, yes. Yes, he's upstairs. He's been here about ten minutes. Seems a bit impatient.

JAMES: Yes, well we'll have to wait a bit longer. I'm going to deal with the Frazer problem first. Who was that well-dressed piece I saw coming out of here as I pulled in?

WHITE: Oh, I don't know …

JAMES: What did she want?

WHITE: Just came in for a drink, that's all …

TUG: Journalist – from London.

JAMES looks immediately suspicious.

TUG: Says she's writin' an article about local personalities. I told her to try the coffee bar under the bridge.

WHITE: She said she'd like to see you.

JAMES: Yes, well, I certainly don't want to see her. If she comes around again get rid of her quick. Understand?

WHITE: Okay.

TUG: Said she'd call back later.

JAMES motions to WHITE. WHITE nods and crosses to the window, looking out.

JAMES: I'm expecting somebody, Tug.

TUG: Right. (*He finishes his drink*)

JAMES: Drop in later. About an hour's time. I may have a job for you.

TUG nods and moves to the door.

JAMES: Not yet. Take a good look at this man – then beat it.

TUG: I get it.

WHITE: (*From the window*) He's just coming down the street.

JAMES: (*To TUG*) Now take a good look and make sure you'll recognise him again.

TUG sits at the bar. JAMES sits at a table. The door opens and FRAZER enters. WHITE turns the sign on the window to CLOSED. TUG rises and crosses to the door. WHITE opens it for him.

TUG: Ta ta for now, mate.

TUG goes out. WHITE locks the door and crosses to the bar and out into the kitchen.

JAMES: You didn't lose much time, Mr Frazer.

FRAZER: My friends are anxious to close the deal.

JAMES: (*Smiling*) I imagined they would be. I hope they appreciate they're getting a bargain.

FRAZER: I don't know about that. I do know they want to see something just a little more convincing than a photograph before they part with their money.

JAMES: What do you mean?

FRAZER: I've got to see Lander and identify him.

JAMES: And then what?

FRAZER: And then you get the money, Mr James.

JAMES: Fifty thousand.

FRAZER: (*Nodding*) That's what you said.

JAMES: (*After a moment*) How long will it take you to get the money?

FRAZER: It depends how you want it.

JAMES: You know how I want it – cash.

FRAZER: Two or three hours.

JAMES ponders for a moment, then comes to a decision.

JAMES: D'you know a place called Craig Park?

FRAZER: No, I don't.

JAMES: You take the Cardiff road – from Melynfforest, that is – and it's about fifteen miles. Half a dozen houses, a pub and a corner shop.

FRAZER: Craig Park.

JAMES: I'll meet you outside the pub there at twelve tomorrow morning.

FRAZER: (*After a slight hesitation*) All right. Tomorrow morning.

JAMES: Well – that's that. Cigarette?

FRAZER: Thank you.

JAMES fumbles for his matches. FRAZER studies him.

FRAZER: Tell me something …

JAMES: Yes?

FRAZER: When you photographed Lander in my overcoat, did you go all the way to Craig Park?

128

JAMES smiles.

FRAZER: After all, if you say it's fifteen miles from Melynfforest …

JAMES: No, Mr Frazer. I didn't go to Craig Park. I just went around the corner here. We move him around, you see. We move him around.

JAMES strikes a match and holds it out for FRAZER to light his cigarette. FRAZER looks at him. He leans forward to accept the light.

CUT TO: The Terrace at St Bride's. Day.

It is the following morning.

ELWYN ROBERTS is seated, reading a newspaper. DR VINCENT stands examining his golf clubs and trying to make conversation with ROBERTS.

VINCENT: … So I took the caddy's advice and used the iron – and what do you think happened?

ROBERTS: (*Bored*) You holed in one.

VINCENT: Good heavens, no! It was four hundred yards … I sliced it out of the bunker and right into the cleft of a tree.

ROBERTS: How clever of you.

VINCENT: Clever? Do you know how many strokes I took on that hole?

ROBERTS: No: Please tell me.

VINCENT: Nine!

ROBERTS: You must have been a very worried man.

FRAZER appears from inside the house.

FRAZER: Lovely morning, gentlemen.

VINCENT: Ah, Frazer …

FRAZER: Anything exciting in the paper this morning, Mr Roberts?

ROBERTS: Er? Oh, no – no, not really. Er – if you'll
            excuse me, I've got several letters to write
            before lunch.

ROBERTS goes into the house.

VINCENT: Something wrong with that fellow.

FRAZER: He's ill?

VINCENT: Liverish, if you ask me. A few rounds of
            golf'd do him the world of good.

FRAZER: Is that what you usually prescribe, Doctor?

VINCENT: Finest cure in the world for anything. Fresh
            air, exercise, congenial company. You can't
            beat it. Are you going into town, Mr Frazer?

FRAZER: Yes. Can I give you a lift down to the course?

VINCENT: Oh – er – no, thanks. I've got a phone call to
            make, and my friends will be here any
            minute.

FRAZER: I'll be getting along then.

VINCENT: A round or two wouldn't do you any harm,
            either …

FRAZER: I'll keep that in mind. Good morning, Doctor.

VINCENT: Morning.

FRAZER walks towards the drive.

CUT TO: A Country Road. Day.

*TUG WALLIS is standing by a telephone box. He is
obviously expecting a call. A lorry is parked some twenty
yards down the road. AL CROSS, a rugged, tough looking
customer, is seated in the driving cab, smoking. He leans
out, looking in TUG WALLIS's direction. TUG gestures
despairingly. Just as he does so, the telephone rings inside
the box. TUG sticks up a thumb to AL CROSS and goes
inside the box, grabbing the receiver. He talks excitedly for
a few seconds and as he does so AL CROSS gets down from*

the lorry and walks along to the telephone box. TUG
WALLIS slams down the receiver and comes out of the box.

TUG: Righto, Al. He's on his way here. Let's get back to
　　　 the lorry.

TUG and AL CROSS start to walk back to the lorry.

CUT TO: Another section of Country Road. Day.

FRAZER's car is driving along the section of road towards
Carreg Bend.

CUT TO: Carreg Bend. Day.

The lorry is now parked on the grass verge facing Carreg
Bend.

CUT TO: Inside the Lorry Cabin. Day.

AL is sitting behind the wheel. TUG is seated beside him.

AL: Who is this poor devil, anyway?

TUG: Never mind who he is. You'll get your cut.

AL: (*Nervously*) Now wait a minute! If this chap is a
　　　 rozzer, I'm not a bit keen on …

TUG: He's not a copper.

AL: Who is he then?

TUG: Al, what the hell does it matter to you what he is …
　　　 you're making two 'undred quid out of this lark!

CUT TO: Carreg Bend. Day.

The lorry is seen on one side of the bend. FRAZER's car is
seen approaching in the distance on the other side.

CUT TO: Inside the Lorry Cabin. Day.

AL is sitting behind the wheel. TUG is seated beside him.

TUG: Any minute now. Start her up.

AL starts the engine. The starter misses.

AL: Blast!

TUG: What's wrong?

AL: All right, all right – don't panic.

AL adjusts the choke and tries again: the engine starts.
TUG WALLIS is relieved.

TUG: (*Tensely*) Now remember. Hit him broadside on as
       he comes round the corner. The second I give the
       word – step on it.

AL nods and revs the engine.

CUT TO: The Country Road. Day.
*FRAZER's car comes into shot driving towards the bend
and the as yet unseen lorry.*

END OF EPISODE FIVE

EPISODE SIX

OPEN TO: The Country Road. Day.
The lorry is on the grass verge with its engine running.

CUT TO: Inside the Lorry Cabin. Day.
AL is sitting behind the wheel. TUG is seated beside him.
They are waiting for FRAZER's car to turn the corner.

AL: We shall be in a hell of a mess if we hit the wrong
        car.

TUG: Don't worry; I'd know him anywhere – and the car.

AL: Yes, I know, but supposing there's another car
        exactly like …

TUG: Al, stop sweating it out, for God's sake! Now just
        do what I tell you. As soon as I give the word, hit
        him for six!

CUT TO: The Country Road. Day.
A car driven by RITA COLMAN passes from behind the
lorry and continues down the road in the direction of the
corner.

CUT TO: Inside the Lorry Cabin. Day.
RITA's car is now visible through the lorry's windscreen
moving towards the corner.

TUG: I know that woman!

AL: (*Anxiously*) Who is she?

TUG: She's a reporter on … (*Angrily*) What the hell's she
        doing here?

CUT TO: The Country Road. Day.
Suddenly, through the windscreen of FRAZER's car, we see
RITA COLMAN turn the corner and approach him. RITA
pulls her car into the side of the road and – jumping out of
the car – rushes towards FRAZER, holding up her hand for

him to stop. FRAZER immediately pulls up and RITA quickly crosses to his car.

RITA: (*Out of breath*) Oh, thank goodness!

FRAZER: Hello, Miss Colman! You seem pretty excited! What's the trouble?

RITA: (*Excited; still out of breath*) Mr Frazer, there's two men round the corner in a lorry … They're going to smash into your car and …

FRAZER: Now wait a minute! (*Smiling*) Take a deep breath. (*After a moment*) Now what's this all about?

RITA: There's two men in a lorry … they're waiting for you just round the corner … They're going to smash into your car …

FRAZER: Are you sure about this?

RITA: Yes! Yes, I'm quite sure! You think I'm talking nonsense, don't you? But I swear I'm not, Mr Frazer, because …

FRAZER interrupts Rita; shaking his head.

FRAZER: No, I don't think you're talking nonsense.

FRAZER leans across and opens the passenger seat door.

FRAZER: You'd better jump in!

RITA: But what about my car?

FRAZER: Don't worry about that! We'll pick that up later. Come along, jump in!

RITA gets into the car. FRAZER, with RITA COLMAN beside him, turns his car round and drives off in the opposite direction.

CUT TO: A secluded country lane. Day.
FRAZER's car pulls onto the grass verge and stops.

136

CUT TO: Inside FRAZER's Car. Day.

FRAZER is just switching off the engine. He turns to face RITA COLMAN.

FRAZER: Now, what's this all about?

RITA: Are you sure we weren't followed?

FRAZER: Yes – don't worry about that. Now tell me about that lorry. Did you know it was going to be there – waiting for me?

RITA: Yes, I did.

FRAZER: How did you know?

RITA: Well, yesterday afternoon, I had a hunch. I followed Elwyn Roberts to Cardiff. He went to the Tiger Bay district – to a place called The Kowloon.

FRAZER: (*Surprised*) I know The Kowloon. I was there myself yesterday. But when did Roberts arrive?

RITA: He got there first, before you and Laurence James.

FRAZER: But he wasn't in the bar.

RITA: I know he wasn't. He was upstairs, waiting for James.

FRAZER: I seem to have under-rated you, Miss Colman. Go on …

RITA: Well, I couldn't hang about The Kowloon very long without becoming conspicuous, so I went to a coffee bar and later to a pub. While I was in the pub, I overheard a conversation between a real tough character called Tug something or other and a lorry driver. Your car was mentioned and Carreg Bend … I put two and two together, Mr Frazer.

FRAZER: Yes, well thank goodness you did, Miss Colman – I only just hired this car.

FRAZER puts his hand on the car key: about to start the car.

RITA: Yes, but just a minute …

FRAZER: Yes?

RITA: You told me that you were down here on business – that you represent the British Research Corporation.

FRAZER: That's right …

RITA: Well, if that's true – why on earth should these people want to kill you?

FRAZER: Oh – you know how it is, Miss Colman.

RITA: I don't know how it is!

FRAZER: Competition is very fierce these days.

FRAZER stares at RITA and starts the car.

CUT TO: The Bar and Lounge of The Kowloon Hotel.

The bar is closed. LAURENCE JAMES and TUG WALLIS are in the middle of a heated argument.

JAMES: … You bungled the whole thing, Tug. Why the devil don't you admit it?

TUG: I tell you the car never came round the corner.

JAMES: It must have done!

TUG: I tell you it didn't!

JAMES: Then what the hell happened to it?

TUG: Don't ask me! I don't know what happened to it! Perhaps that woman tipped him off, or he got wise to things. (*A shrug*) I just don't know! Anyway, what I want to know is who pays my mate for losing a day's work with the lorry?

ROGER THORNTON comes in from the street. He closes the door behind him and stands looking at TUG and LAURENCE JAMES. JAMES takes out his wallet and gives TUG some money.

JAMES: All right – here you are. And mind you keep
              your mouth shut. I'll be in touch.

*TUG nods, puts the money in his pocket, and with a curious
glance at THORNTON goes out into the street.
THORNTON moves towards JAMES.*

JAMES: (*Looking at THORNTON with interest*) You
              look as if you need a drink.

THORNTON: No – I don't want a drink. Not at the
              moment.

JAMES: (*Offering his cigarette case*) Well, have a
              cigarette. You certainly need something to
              calm you down.

THORNTON: Larry, I'm worried. I'm very worried about
              this Kurt Lander business.

JAMES: Well, if you want easy money, you've got to
              be prepared to take risks.

THORNTON: In my opinion, Roberts has made a good
              offer and we should accept it.

JAMES: Forty thousand isn't enough – Lander's
              worth more than forty thousand.

THORNTON: That may be – but so far as I'm concerned
              this business is getting out of hand …

JAMES: What do you mean?

THORNTON: Well – take this chap Frazer …

JAMES: Frazer? What about Frazer?

THORNTON: I think he's working with the police, I'm
              sure of it in fact. I've felt it ever since I got
              rid of Eve Turner.

JAMES: Yes, well – getting rid of that girl was a
              mistake! I said so at the time. (*Shaking his
              head*) You shouldn't have done it.

THORNTON: I'd no idea she carried that damned knife.
              When she went for me like that, I had to do
              something. It was her or me.

JAMES: Yes, well I still think it was a mistake.
                However, go on – what else do you know
                about Frazer?

THORNTON: A couple of days ago, when I was out
                surveying a property, I saw Frazer sitting on
                a riverbank talking to a man whose face was
                vaguely familiar. I couldn't think where I'd
                seen him before, then suddenly I
                remembered. It was in Frankfurt at the end
                of the war. He was a big noise in Army
                Intelligence. His name was Lockwood.

JAMES looks at THORNTON, obviously interested by this
information.

JAMES: Are you sure about this?

THORNTON: Yes, I'm quite sure.

JAMES: You're not just making this up because you
                want me to accept the Roberts offer?

THORNTON: No, of course I'm not. I swear I'm not,
                Larry!

JAMES hesitates a moment, then turns towards the table
and stubs out his cigarette.

JAMES: I don't like this. I don't like the sound of it.

THORNTON: No, I didn't think you would!

JAMES: (*Quietly. After a moment*) All right. We'll
                play for safety. Telephone Roberts and tell
                him it's a deal. He can pick up Lander on
                Thursday night.

THORNTON nods: he is obviously relieved.

CUT TO: The Lounge at St Bride's Guest House. Day.
FRAZER is standing in the middle of the room. He wears an
overcoat, unbuttoned and his suitcases are on the floor
beside him. MRS CRICHTON is just giving him a receipted
bill.

140

MRS CRICHTON:	… There's your receipt, Mr Frazer. I think you'll find it's all in order.
FRAZER:	(*Glancing at it*) Thank you, Mrs Crichton.
MRS CRICHTON:	I'm sorry you couldn't stay a little longer, especially now that the weather is improving.
FRAZER:	I'm sorry, too. I've been very comfortable here.
MRS CRICHTON:	Well, thank you, Mr Frazer. If ever you should get an opportunity to recommend …
FRAZER:	(*Smiling*) Don't worry, Mrs Crichton. I will. If it were left to me, I'd stay another week or two, but my firm's decided to send me up to Scotland.
MRS CRICHTON:	Scotland?
FRAZER:	Yes, they seem to think there's more scope up there.
MRS CRICHTON:	Well, I'm sure they must know their own business best; and I must say I'm terribly relieved to hear that we're not going to get any of those horrible little factories popping up all over the place.

FRAZER smiles. DR VINCENT comes in from the terrace carrying his golf clubs.

VINCENT:	Hello! Somebody moving on?
FRAZER:	Yes, I'm afraid so.
VINCENT:	Well, well, that's a pity – a great pity. I thought I was going to make a golfer out of you.
FRAZER:	Maybe I'll be back one of these days.
MRS CRICHTON:	I'm sure we all hope to see Mr Frazer again some time.

VINCENT:	Going far, Frazer?
FRAZER:	Scotland.
VINCENT:	Ah, some splendid courses up there – really magnificent! I remember a holiday I had in Perth in '48, it was one of the best …
FRAZER:	(*Interrupting VINCENT*) I don't suppose I'll get much time for recreation.
VINCENT:	(*Shaking his head*) You'll come round to it in time, dear boy! Do you the world of good. Ah, well, I must get my bath.

VINCENT shakes hands with FRAZER.

| VINCENT: | Goodbye, Mr Frazer. |
| FRAZER: | Goodbye, Doctor. |

VINCENT goes.

| MRS CRICHTON: | Is your car ready, Mr Frazer? |
| FRAZER: | Yes, it's out in the drive. If you'll say goodbye to the others for me … |

AS FRAZER speaks ELWYN ROBERTS comes in. He is taking off his cap and carries a walking stick.

MRS CRICHTON:	Ah, here's Mr Roberts …
ROBERTS:	Just walked as far as the flagstaff and … Hello – are you leaving, Mr Frazer?
FRAZER:	Yes, I have to go up to Scotland for a couple of weeks, I'm afraid.
ROBERTS:	Scotland? Well, well … I'm sorry to hear that. We were getting to know you. And I must say I never had a more tolerant neighbour in that room of yours.
FRAZER:	I've enjoyed your music.

ROBERTS:	(*Laughing*) You're the first, Mr Frazer – the very first.

DAVY WILLIAMS puts his head round the door.

DAVY:	Ah, there you are, Mr Roberts! Telephone …
ROBERTS:	For me? Who is it?
DAVY:	A Captain Stribling, or Kipling, or some such name. I didn't quite get it.
ROBERTS:	(*Smiling*) Oh, Captain Stribling. (*Shaking his head*) Really, these people who use their army titles. (*To FRAZER*) He's the gentleman who keeps trying to interest me in a television set. Persistent devil!
MRS CRICHTON:	(*Alarmed*) Television!
ROBERTS:	It's all right, Mrs Crichton. I haven't the slightest intention of buying one.

ROBERTS shakes hands with FRAZER.

ROBERTS:	Well, goodbye, Mr Frazer. Pleasant journey.
FRAZER:	Goodbye, Mr Roberts.

ROBERTS goes out to the telephone.

FRAZER:	Well, I'd better be on my way, Mrs Crichton.

FRAZER picks up his suitcases.

MRS CRICHTON:	Davy can carry those for you, Mr Frazer.
FRAZER:	That's all right, Mrs Crichton. I can manage.

FRAZER smiles at MRS CRICHTON and crosses towards the door.

FRAZER:	Goodbye, Mrs Crichton, and thank you very much.

CUT TO: The Library, 29 Smith Square, London, S.W.1. Day

ROSS is on the telephone. MAJOR LOCKWOOD sits facing the desk, watching him.

ROSS: … Yes, I've got the file. It's just been delivered. And Hobson – I don't want any more calls for the next half hour or so … Yes, of course – send Frazer in the moment he arrives. (*He replaces the receiver*)

LOCKWOOD: Does Frazer know the full story, sir?

ROSS: Not yet. (*Smiling*) I'm only just gathering up the odds and ends myself. (*He opens the file and picks up a document*)

LOCKWOOD: How far have you got?

ROSS: Well, it all started when Miss Thackeray arranged for Kurt Lander to escape from China. Unfortunately, Laurence James persuaded Lander that his rescuers were a bunch of crooks and that they intended to hold him to ransom.

LOCKWOOD: And Lander fell for that?

ROSS: He certainly did – so much so that James provided him with an American passport and brought him to Wales.

LOCKWOOD: Did James have any political affiliations?

ROSS: None whatever.

LOCKWOOD: I see. He was prepared to sell Lander to the highest bidder.

ROSS: That's right.

LOCKWOOD: Meanwhile, Miss Thackeray realised what had happened and came chasing back to Wales under the name of Bradford.

ROSS: Correct. Very soon afterwards James and Thornton, who had planned the Lander operation, began to wonder why the mysterious Miss Bradford had arrived in Melynfforest. They sent Eve Turner to Hong Kong to make inquiries. When she reported that the music teacher had disappeared, they guessed that Miss Bradford was in fact Miss Thackeray.

LOCKWOOD: Yes. But what made Eve Turner turn up at London Airport in Miss Thackeray's place?

ROSS: She didn't.

LOCKWOOD: What?

ROSS: You mistook her for our Miss Thackeray. When Eve Turner didn't find Miss Thackeray in Hong Kong she discovered that a passage had been booked in her name with B.O.A.C. Eve Turner booked on the same plane.

LOCKWOOD: In the hope that Thackeray might be on it.

ROSS: Exactly. But she wasn't, of course. The booking was a 'blind' – she was already over here.

LOCKWOOD: Yes, but what about that tape recording?

ROSS: Eve Turner found it when she was going through Thackeray's flat in Hong

	Kong. She brought it back so that James could compare Thackeray's voice with Miss Bradford's.
LOCKWOOD:	I see. And in the meantime, James had taken the law into his own hands and disposed of Miss Thackeray?
ROSS:	Yes. It's my guess, James followed her to Tregarn Cottage one night and overheard a telephone conversation with one of her contacts. After killing her, he sent Eve Turner to the cottage to take the calls. That's how she ran into Frazer and lost her head.

There is a knock on the door and FRAZER enters. He carries a briefcase.

FRAZER:	Good afternoon, sir. Sorry I'm late.
ROSS:	That's all right, Frazer.
FRAZER:	(*To LOCKWOOD*) When did you drag yourself away from the river?
LOCKWOOD:	I came up last night. I had a meeting at the Yard.
ROSS:	We've had to pull them in on this business, I'm afraid. They insisted because of the Turner murder.
FRAZER:	(*Nodding: opening his briefcase*) I rather thought that would happen.
ROSS:	Is there any news?

FRAZER takes a recording tape out of the case.

FRAZER:	Yes. Thornton telephoned Roberts this morning, just after breakfast. I had the call taped, sir.
ROSS:	Good. Have you got it with you?
FRAZER:	Yes.
ROSS:	Let's hear it.

LOCKWOOD: I'll do it.

ROSS: Do you think Roberts believed your story about Scotland?

FRAZER: I don't know. It's difficult to tell. He appeared to believe it.

ROSS: M'm. What about the others at the guest house?

FRAZER: Oh. I think they swallowed it all right. Mrs Crichton certainly did.

ROSS: (*Nodding: To LOCKWOOD*) Ready?

LOCKWOOD: Yes, sir.

LOCKWOOD presses the recorder switch, and the tape starts turning. We hear the ringing out tone and then the sound of a telephone receiver being lifted, followed by the recorded voices of ROGER THORNTON and ROBERTS. We hear various switchboard noises and then the sound of an extension receiver being lifted:

THORNTON: Mr Elwyn Roberts?

ROBERTS: Speaking …

THORNTON: This is Roger Thornton, Mr Roberts, the estate agent …

ROBERTS: Oh, yes. Good morning, Mr Thornton.

THORNTON: Good morning, sir. I've got some good news for you.

ROBERTS: I'm delighted to hear it.

THORNTON: You know that property you were enquiring about …?

ROBERTS: Yes, yes, of course …

THORNTON: Well, my client's finally reached a decision, sir. He's prepared to accept your offer of forty thousand.

ROBERTS: Oh. Oh, I see. Well – in that case we'd better arrange a meeting.

THORNTON: I've suggested Thursday evening, sir – seven o'clock.

ROBERTS: Where?

THORNTON: The Kowloon Hotel. Is that convenient?

ROBERTS: Yes – yes, that's all right.

THORNTON: (*Hesitant*) You remember our little discussion about the financial arrangements with regard …

ROBERTS: (*Cutting THORNTON short*) Yes, I do indeed. Don't worry – that will be taken care of. Thursday night, seven o'clock?

THORNTON: Yes, that's right …

ROBERTS: Thank you, Mr Thornton.

THORNTON: Thank you, sir.

There is the sound of the telephone receiver being replaced. LOCKWOOD switches off the recorder.

ROSS: Well, that seems pretty clear – unless there's a slip-up.

FRAZER: Or a change of plan at the last moment.

ROSS looks at FRAZER.

ROSS: (*Quietly*) Yes. Lockwood, I want you to have another word with Superintendent Nash. Let him hear that tape.

LOCKWOOD: Yes, sir.

ROSS: Get the whole layout for Thursday night quite clear. Tell Nash to bring the Glamorganshire police in on it, as well as Cardiff. Whatever happens we don't want any slip-ups. (*To FRAZER*) And Frazer, I want you to make a careful check on all outward shipping from Cardiff in the next forty-eight hours.

FRAZER takes a folded paper from his pocket and puts it on the desk in front of ROSS.

FRAZER: Here comes my promotion, sir, I've already done it.

ROSS gives FRAZER a quizzical look and picks up the sheet of paper. LOCKWOOD smiles to himself.

CUT TO: The Entrance to a bank in a Cardiff main street. Day.

ELWYN ROBERTS comes out of the main entrance to the bank, looks up and down the street, then crosses to a stationary car. He is carrying an attaché case.

CUT TO: The Bar and Lounge of The Kowloon Hotel. Night.

ROBERTS and THORNTON are sitting at a table. The attaché case is on the table in front of ROBERTS. With a gesture of annoyance, ROBERTS looks at his wristlet watch, then across at the clock. THORNTON is worried and a little tense.

ROBERTS: It's 7.45 already – where the devil is he?

THORNTON: I'm sorry about this.

ROBERTS: Not so sorry as I am!

THORNTON: When I spoke to him this morning, he said there'd be no trouble in getting Lander here for seven o'clock.

ROBERTS: I like people to be punctual – especially when there's an element of risk attached to the transaction.

THORNTON: He'll be here, don't worry …

ROBERTS: I've got exactly an hour before the boat sails. (*He rises*) I was a fool. I should have stipulated that Lander was brought straight to the boat.

THORNTON: You'll have plenty of time. It won't take ten minutes to get you to the docks.

ROBERTS: (*Looking at THORNTON*) You sound more
            optimistic than you look, Mr Thornton. (*He
            glances at his watch again*) I'm going to
            give your friend exactly fifteen minutes.
            Then, if he isn't here by eight o'clock …

ROBERTS stops talking and looks towards the window.
There is the sound of a car pulling up outside the hotel.
THORNTON crosses to the window.

THORNTON: (*Looking out of the window*) Here he is!

CUT TO: Street in Tiger Bay. Outside The Kowloon
Hotel. Night.

LAURENCE JAMES is getting out of the Mercedes car. He
looks up and down the street and then opens one of the rear
doors of the car. KURT LANDER is slumped unconscious in
the back seat. He has been drugged. JAMES leans forward
and pulls back one of LANDER's eyelids. He nods to
himself, obviously satisfied, then he slightly changes
LANDER's position on the seat. After a moment he closes
the door of the car and goes into the hotel.

CUT TO: The Bar and Lounge of The Kowloon Hotel.
Night.

THORNTON turns from the window and crosses to where
ROBERTS is standing. JAMES enters.

JAMES: (*To ROBERTS*) Good evening …
ROBERTS: You said seven o'clock …
JAMES: Yes, I know. The doctor was late.
ROBERTS: (*Surprised*) What doctor?
JAMES: Have you got the money?
ROBERTS: I said: what doctor?
JAMES: We had trouble with Lander – we had to
            give him an injection.
ROBERTS: (*Annoyed*) You bloody fool!

JAMES: It's all right – don't panic. The doctor's in
              my pocket. If he so much as opens his
              mouth he's had it, and he knows that. Now
              where's the money? (*Pointing to the attaché
              case*) Is that it?

ROBERTS: Yes.

THORNTON: (*To JAMES*) It's all right – I've checked it.

ROBERTS: Where's Lander – in the car?

JAMES: Yes.

ROBERTS: How long will he be out?

JAMES: About four hours.

ROBERTS: All right. Let's get going.

JAMES looks at the attaché case.

JAMES: (*To THORNTON*) There's no need for you
              to come. I'll be back in twenty minutes.
              Take the money.

ROBERTS: (*Picks up the case*) We're all going.

JAMES: What do you mean? What's the idea?

ROBERTS: You heard what I said. We're all going.

JAMES: But that's ridiculous, there's no need …

ROBERTS: I'll hand this over when we reach the docks
              – not until.

JAMES: You're not taking any chances, are you, Mr
              Roberts?

ROBERTS: No. You've pulled the wool over my eyes
              once; you're not going to do it again.

THORNTON: What do you mean?

ROBERTS: You know damn well what I mean!

JAMES: (*To THORNTON: highly amused*) He didn't
              realise Steinbeck was Kurt Lander. The
              clothes and the white hair fooled him.
              (*Laughing*) He was staying under the same
              roof and he didn't …

ROBERTS: (*Angry*) All right, all right! I didn't know much about Lander then, I hadn't a proper description of him.

ROBERTS grabs hold of JAMES by the lapel of his overcoat.

ROBERTS: But I've got one now, Mr James – so don't try and sell me a pup!

JAMES pushes ROBERTS away from him.

JAMES: Lander's outside; judge for yourself …

CUT TO: The Street in Tiger Bay. Outside The Kowloon Hotel. Night.

JAMES comes out followed by ROBERTS and ROGER THORNTON. They cross quite briskly to the Mercedes car. JAMES opens the back door of the car for ROBERTS to look inside.

ROBERTS takes a look at KURT LANDER, then withdraws his head and nods to JAMES, who closes the back door and opens the driving door. JAMES has one foot inside the car when suddenly all three turn and look behind them. They see an approaching police car.

THORNTON: (*Scared*) What the hell's happening?

They look in the opposite direction and see a second police car approaching from the other end of the street. Another car pulls up behind this and uniformed and plain-clothes men pour into the street. FRAZER, LOCKWOOD, INSPECTOR ROYD are included in this group, and SUPERINTENDENT NASH.

THORNTON turns to go back into the hotel. Two plain-clothes detectives are approaching the doorway. JAMES moves a few yards towards an alley. Two detectives are waiting for him.

JAMES and THORNTON suddenly dash across the road and make for a bombed site on a piece of waste ground. The police are close behind them. More police appear, to cut them off. Two plain-clothes men from the hotel are within a few yards of ROBERTS when he whips out a revolver, opens the back door of the car, and fires point blank at LANDER; as the detectives rush up to him, he dives between them and gets back into the hotel.

SUPERINTENDENT NASH, FRAZER and LOCKWOOD join the detectives looking at LANDER in the Mercedes. Police are pouring into the hotel in pursuit of ROBERTS. NASH speaks to an officer.

NASH: An ambulance – quick!

FRAZER: (*To LOCKWOOD*) Keep an eye on him. I'll take the hotel!

FRAZER goes into the hotel. INSPECTOR ROYD joins NASH and LOCKWOOD.

ROYD: (*To NASH*) They've got two of them in the next road.

ROYD indicates LANDER.

ROYD: How is he?

LOCKWOOD: Pretty bad, I should imagine.

Two police constables dash into the hotel.

CUT TO: The Bar and Lounge of The Kowloon Hotel. Night.

The two police constables enter from the street as FRAZER comes out of the kitchen from behind the bar.

CONSTABLE: Have you seen him, sir?

FRAZER: No … He's not through there!

As FRAZER speaks a man's voice can be heard shouting from the top of the staircase.

MAN: (*Off*) He's on the roof!

FRAZER, followed by the two policemen, dash towards the staircase.

CUT TO: Rooftops in the Tiger Bay area of Cardiff. Night.

ELWYN ROBERTS comes into sight from behind a chimney and climbs over a parapet. He seems worried, appears dishevelled, and still carries his revolver and the attaché case. He looks over his shoulder two or three times as he works his way towards the camera.

CUT TO: The Street in Tiger Bay. Outside The Kowloon Hotel. Night.

Ambulance attendants are just putting a stretcher, bearing KURT LANDER, into a stationary ambulance. LOCKWOOD is standing talking to a middle-aged DOCTOR. INSPECTOR ROYD comes out of the hotel.

ROYD: (*To LOCKWOOD*) What's the score?

LOCKWOOD indicates the DOCTOR.

DOCTOR: (*A shrug*) I've given him a blood transfusion. We'll know more later.

LOCKWOOD: (*To ROYD*) Have they got Roberts?

ROYD: Not yet, but I've just had a message that the other two are being brought in.

LOCKWOOD nods.

CUT TO: Rooftops in Tiger Bay. Night.

ROBERTS has pocketed the gun so he can use both hands when jumping over a narrow gap between two buildings. He negotiates this and turns to see FRAZER about to do the same.

Just as FRAZER is about to jump ROBERTS throws the attaché case at him. The case hits him and bursts open. Bundles of bank notes fall into the street below. FRAZER falls back and almost loses his balance but recovers.

CUT TO: Tiger Bay. Night.
The attaché case and bank notes fall from the roof.

CUT TO: Rooftops in Tiger Bay. Night.
ELWYN ROBERTS has found a skylight and is in the process of forcing it open; he finally succeeds and climbs through into the room below.

CUT TO: A Lumber Room, with skylight, in a warehouse. Night.
There is rubbish of all sorts scattered around the room.
ROBERTS comes through the skylight and lowers himself onto a piece of junk furniture. He pauses for a moment and then, after pushing a piece of wood under the skylight, he clambers down.

CUT TO: Rooftops in Tiger Bay. Night.
FRAZER is trying desperately to force open the skylight. After a moment he realises this is an impossible task and rises to his feet. He looks at his watch, hesitates a moment, then returns across the rooftops.

CUT TO: The Warehouse. Night.
ELWYN ROBERTS descends a flight of rickety stairs. He is now on the ground floor, moving along a passage towards a door. He opens the door, peers out, then goes out into the narrow street.

CUT TO: A narrow alley in Tiger Bay. Night.
A door slowly opens, and ROBERTS emerges. He looks continuously up and down the alley, then makes off quickly in the direction of the main street.

155

CUT TO: A Street in Tiger Bay. Night.

ROBERTS is standing on the corner of the street, undecided which way to go. A police car approaches. ROBERTS suddenly sees it and makes off in the opposite direction.

CUT TO: Inside the Police Car. Night.

The Police Officer, sitting beside the driver, sees ROBERTS in the distance through the windscreen. He points to him and the driver nods. The car continues to pursue the retreating figure of ELWYN ROBERTS.

CUT TO: A Street in Tiger Bay. Night.

ROBERTS is running away from the police car. The car is held up by traffic. Eventually the traffic clears, and the police continue in pursuit of the retreating ROBERTS.

CUT TO: Dockside Railway siding in Tiger Bay. Night.

Coal and cargo trucks are being shunted into position for loading and unloading onto various tramp steamers.

A gang of youths – teddy boys – are fooling about near the trucks throwing pieces of coal at each other. Playing each other up.

ROBERTS suddenly appears, pursued by the police car. The gang stop their fooling and stare at ROBERTS and the police car in amazement.

ROBERTS makes a quick dash in the direction of the stationary trucks as the police car brakes to a standstill. LOCKWOOD and the police pour out of the car in pursuit of ROBERTS.

ROBERTS reaches the gang of teddy boys and suddenly grabs one of them by the arm and drags him across the railway track. The youth is completely taken by surprise and it is several seconds before he finally realises what has happened and starts to struggle in an attempt to free himself.

ROBERTS points the revolver at the boy's head and shouts across at LOCKWOOD and the approaching police:

ROBERTS: I'll blow his bloody head off if you come a step nearer!

LOCKWOOD and the police stop dead. The youth is terrified now; staring at ROBERTS open-mouthed. The rest of the gang are frightened, their movements literally frozen. Suddenly a row of trucks are shunted between ROBERTS and the police, cutting off our vision of ROBERTS and the frightened youth. LOCKWOOD and the police rush towards the trucks with the object of cautiously edging their way around the trucks.

CUT TO: Dockside Railway Siding in Tiger Bay. Night.

LOCKWOOD and the police emerge from behind the trucks, which have now come to a standstill. There is no sign of ROBERTS.

The youth is sitting on the floor, holding his head – dazed and confused. It is obvious that ROBERTS has knocked him out. LOCKWOOD dashes up to him and says:

LOCKWOOD: Where is he?

The boy shakes his head; bewildered. The police race towards another section of the siding in search of ROBERTS.

CUT TO: A dock in the Tiger Bay area of Cardiff. Night.

The Uganda, a tramp steamer, is shortly to sail and is sounding its sirens. ROBERTS emerges from the shadows and amidst the general confusion pushes his way through a group of seamen.

CUT TO: The Deck of the Tramp Steamer. Night.

ROBERTS is standing by the deckhouse, talking to the ship's captain. The captain is looking at him with curiosity for ROBERTS looks distinctly dishevelled and exhausted.

STRIBLING: I gave you up as a bad job, sir. I expected you and your friend over an hour ago.

ROBERTS: Yes, I know. I'm sorry, Captain Stribling … but unfortunately …

ROBERTS has difficulty getting his breath.

STRIBLING: (*Quietly*) Go on, sir …

ROBERTS: My friend couldn't make it. He was taken ill.

STRIBLING: Oh, I'm sorry to hear that. (*Looking at ROBERTS*) If you don't mind my saying so, you don't look too good either, sir.

ROBERTS: No, I – I'm not a hundred per cent. I've had a pretty hectic time. (*Forcing a smile*) Been living it up a bit – you know how it is.

STRIBLING: Yes. Well, if I were you, I'd go and lie down for a while. It's the first cabin on the left. Number one.

ROBERTS: (*Nodding: relieved*) Thank you, Captain.

ROBERTS goes through a door. CAPTAIN STRIBLING turns to speak to one of his crew.

CUT TO: The Companionway of the Tramp Steamer. Night.

Still breathing heavily, ROBERTS approaches, looking at the cabin doors. He finds the cabin he wants, hesitates, then leans against the wall. He takes a handkerchief out of his pocket and mops his forehead. Finally, he turns and opens the cabin door.

CUT TO: The Cabin in the Tramp Steamer. Night.

ROBERTS enters and suddenly he stops dead as he sees FRAZER sitting on the bunk, facing the door, holding a revolver and pointing it at ROBERTS.

FRAZER: Hello, Mr Roberts.

CUT TO: The Library, 29 Smith Square, London. Day.

ROSS is sitting at his desk, writing a letter. He signs it, folds it, and puts it in an envelope. He is addressing the envelope when there is a knock on the door and FRAZER enters.

FRAZER: May I come in, sir?

ROSS: Yes, of course. Come in, Frazer.

ROSS rises and joins FRAZER in front of the desk.

FRAZER: I've just been having a talk to Lockwood; he tells me that Lander came through the operation.

ROSS: Yes, he did, very well.

ROSS indicates the telephone on his desk.

ROSS: The hospital sounded much more optimistic this morning.

FRAZER: Oh, good.

ROSS: (*Pleasantly*) Well, Frazer – you did a good job. I'm very grateful.

FRAZER: Thank you, sir.

ROSS: I understand you're going on leave for two weeks.

FRAZER: Yes, sir. I'm flying down to the South of France. I'm ready to go right now.

ROSS: (*Smiling*) The Sunny Place for Shady People, eh? (*Shaking hands with FRAZER*) Well – have a good time, and don't forget to be back by the 21st.

FRAZER: No, all right, I won't. Have you anything lined up for me when I get back, sir?

159

ROSS turns towards his desk.

FRAZER: Is there something on the cards for the 21st, sir?

ROSS turns and looks at FRAZER.

ROSS: (*With an imperceptible sigh*) In this department, there's always something on the cards, Frazer. Have a good time in the South of France.

FRAZER exits and ROSS turns towards his desk again.

CUT TO: London Airport. Day.

A group of passengers, including FRAZER, are walking towards a B.E.A. aircraft.

CUT TO: Inside the B.E.A. Aircraft. Day.

FRAZER is sitting next to a woman called GINA. They unfasten their safety belts.

GINA: Je n'en comprends pas un mot.

FRAZER: I beg your pardon?

GINA: (*Indicating her book*) I just don't believe a word of it.

FRAZER: No good?

GINA: Oh yes, it's terribly exciting. But so impossible! It's all about a secret agent. Would you like to borrow it?

FRAZER: No thanks. I'll take it as read. Are you going on holiday?

GINA: No, I live in St Tropez. Where are you going?

FRAZER: Juan le … St Tropez.

GINA: Oh, how nice. And what are you going to do in St Tropez, Mr …?

FRAZER: Frazer. Tim Frazer. I'll do some sunbathing and I thought maybe I'd learn to water-ski.

GINA: And why not? It's a wonderful idea. I'll teach you.

FRAZER: You'll teach … Are you a good teacher, Madame?
GINA: Mademoiselle …
FRAZER: Oh, that's nice …
GINA: The teacher depends on the pupil, Mr Frazer. Are you a good pupil?
FRAZER: Oh, I think I'll be a very good pupil, Mademoiselle.

CUT TO: The airplane disappearing into the distance.

THE END

TIM FRAZER
AND THE
MELVIN AFFAIR

A FILM STORY
by
FRANCIS DURBRIDGE

Tim Frazer, a temporarily unemployed engineer who is working as a secret agent, is surprised to receive a summons from Ross, his departmental chief, who arranges a rendezvous at a fashionable night spot called Beverley's.

While they are dining and watching the cabaret, Ross directs Frazer's attention to a singer named Loraine Daly who, he says, is to be the subject of Frazer's next assignment.

He says he wants Frazer to keep a very close watch on the singer, and when Frazer wants to know in what way Loraine is threatened, Ross shows him a report in the evening paper of a woman's body being taken from the river. He says he has every reason to believe that this woman was killed by someone working to orders, and under the impression that his victim was Loraine Daly.

Ross says that Loraine is undoubtedly attracting attention from certain international agents they know, but he cannot be sure of the reason. Possibly it is because she may have picked up some information on her travels across Europe, where she performs extensively.

There is a minor sensation at the end of the singer's act when a paunchy Italian makes a great show of handing her a bouquet. Ross startles Frazer by telling him that this man, Vivaldi, has most probably engineered the attempt on Loraine's life. Ross says he cannot tell Frazer much more at this stage, but gives him carte blanche, saying he need not actually contact the girl unless it is necessary, but he is to keep a very close watch on her.

Frazer waits around the stage door, and when Loraine emerges and enters a chauffeur-driven limousine he follows at a respectable distance. Suddenly, the chauffeur appears to lose control of Loraine's car, which crashes over the kerb and into a shop window. Frazer comes running up, helps Loraine out of the car, then puts out the engine which has caught fire. The chauffeur is dazed and cannot understand what went wrong with the steering. Frazer is inclined to be suspicious, and eventually he takes the girl back to her flat.

Over a drink she confides in Frazer that she has been very worried of late and welcomes the end of her current engagement. She says it is a long time since she had news of her brother, Guy Melvin, a newspaper correspondent last heard of in Yugoslavia. There have been reports that he has gone to Russia and the press have been bothering her. Frazer says he will do anything he can to help.

Frazer reports to Ross by telephone. Ross tells him he knew that Guy Melvin was Loraine's brother, but he cannot be quite certain that this is the reason why enemies are trying to kill her. However, he says he will see her himself the next day and put into operation a plan which will involve Frazer.

When Ross interviews Loraine Daly the following afternoon he shows her a wristwatch, which she at once recognises as her brother's. He tells her the watch came to them from a Canadian agent named Lefferts. Lefferts had been contacted by Loraine's brother in Belgrade. On the inside of the strap was crudely scrawled the message: "The Death's Head Tower at Nis is a must for all tourists." Loraine is as baffled as Ross by this, and eventually agrees to go to Yugoslavia and try to find out what has happened to her brother.

***

On the plane to Trieste, Loraine is surprised to see Frazer, who explains that he is going out there as correspondent of a trade journal to investigate the question of certain engineering exports to Yugoslavia. Frazer gives the same explanation to Vivaldi, who is sitting next to him.

166

Also on the plane is Miss Rowley, a cheerful old lady who tells them that she is an archaeologist on her way to the ancient city of Nis, birthplace of Constantine the Great, where some new excavations are taking place. She adds pleasantly: "The Death Head Tower at Nis is a must for all tourists."

Vivaldi introduces himself to Frazer as director of an oil combine and professes to be a great admirer of Loraine Daly.

***

At the Trieste Hotel Loraine agrees to dine with Frazer, who is late for the rendezvous. While she is waiting she encounters Vivaldi, who gets her a cocktail. As she is about to drink, the glass is knocked from her hand by an affable young German named Kramer, who apologises profusely and gets her another.

Over dinner Frazer tries to get Loraine to talk about her visit to Belgrade the next day, but she refuses to say any more.

On going to her room she is startled to find Kramer there. At first he appears to be threatening and tells her not to switch on the light. Then he admits that he knocked over her glass quite deliberately earlier on, for the simple reason that the drink had been doped. He then reveals that he knows why Loraine is there and says he has met her brother Guy Melvin. Kramer strongly advises her to go back home. When she stubbornly refuses he relents a little, and finally says that if she must go to Belgrade then she should try to find an Englishman who calls himself D'Arcy and who keeps a pet shop just off Sunset Square. D'Arcy had been dropped by parachute into Yugoslavia during the war and had remained there ever since.

167

When she is packing the next morning, Loraine has a visit from Frazer who says he has to go to Belgrade on sudden instructions from his trade journal. She tells him of Kramer's visit, and Frazer tells her that he knows she is looking for her brother. She says she will try to find a man named Peter Lefferts, who has sent the strange message on the wristwatch. He may know something about her brother. Frazer and Loraine try to fathom why Miss Rowley, the archaeologist whom they met on the plane, should have repeated the words of the message.

***

In Belgrade, they have some difficulty in finding the side street off Sunset Square where D'Arcy has his pet shop, but eventually they discover it. Behind a curtain at the far end of the shop they find the body of Miss Rowley.

Frazer sends Loraine back to the car while he searches the body. The car driver says he can take them to the bar frequented by D'Arcy, so they drive there and Frazer seeks out D'Arcy. D'Arcy at first denies that he knows Guy Melvin, but later admits that Guy visited him some months ago to try to buy from him an unusual music-box. The sale did not go through and D'Arcy says he disposed of it to another customer, an American girl named Ella Bates, a hostess at a club called the Villanova.

When Frazer asks if he knows a woman named Miss Rowley, D'Arcy says he doesn't.

After D'Arcy has gone, Vivaldi comes in. He says he has been sightseeing and lost his way.

***

168

Later, when Frazer and Loraine have dined at the hotel, there is still apparently no news of the discovery of Miss Rowley's body. Loraine says she thinks that, although she had not heard from her brother, Vivaldi is probably under the impression that Guy had written to her and sent her some information possibly concerning the music-box – which he (Vivaldi) badly wants; and maybe Kramer and Miss Rowley were also interested in this information.

On the way to the Villanova, the driver goes off the route, and they find a narrow street blocked by a hand-cart. Frazer at once produces a gun and orders the driver to keep going. The hand-cart is smashed, but no one is hurt. Eventually the driver confesses that he had been offered a large sum to drive down that narrow street. Frazer asks him to describe the man who bribed him, expecting to get a description of Vivaldi – but the driver gives a fairly accurate one of Kramer.

Arrived at the Villanova, Frazer gets a table for himself and Loraine, and asks the waiter about Ella Bates. Presently the hostess joins them, and Loraine asks her if she knows Guy Melvin, her brother. Frazer starts to ask her about the music-box, and at first she is exasperated. Finally, she agrees to tell them what she knows about it.

Ella says that Guy Melvin used to drop in regularly at the Villanova at one time and she was quite fond of him. Then D'Arcy came in one night and offered her a substantial bribe to tell certain people that he had bought a valuable music-box and re-sold it at once … to her. When Guy asked her about the music-box, Ella says, she told him that she had sent it to a friend in America who collected them. Obviously Guy didn't believe her. She told the same story to another enquirer – Vivaldi – who said that if she could get the box back from the States he would pay her 12,000 dollars. At the first opportunity Ella went round to see D'Arcy, who laughed at the proposition, saying he would not be interested in ten times the amount. After that, Ella had gone to see Guy Melvin at his hotel, only to be told that he had left.

After Ella has gone, Frazer tells Loraine that he thinks her brother refused to swallow Ella's story of the music-box, and – because he was aware of the real value of the box – has been forcibly detained somewhere.

As they are talking, Peter Lefferts comes in and introduces himself to Loraine, saying he is an acquaintance of Ross. He asks her to dine with him the following evening, when, he says, he will have some information for her. She agrees. Before Lefferts goes he says he would have thought that Ross would have deduced, from the message on the watch, that Guy Melvin was somewhere in Nis. Guy had implied as much to Lefferts when he handed over the watch. He then enlightens them as to the identity of Miss Rowley; she was a British agent, and he says he saw Vivaldi follow her into the pet shop.

When Lefferts has gone there is a slight commotion in the restaurant and Frazer is just in time to save D'Arcy being ejected by an irate proprietor. D'Arcy asks Loraine how she would like to see her brother that night, and says he is to be found in a room over an obscure café called the Flaming Torch. They will recognise it by the sign outside. He tells Frazer to ask for Venizelos.

They go at once to Galicia Street in a poor quarter of the town and eventually find a café with a smoky torch over the door. Then they realise they are being followed.

They wait in an alley, then pounce on the man, who proves to be Vivaldi, whom Frazer deprives of his revolver. He admits the attempts on Loraine's life and to bribing the car driver to implicate Kramer in the last attempt. Frazer is just questioning him about the music-box when a car drives past. There are several shots, one of which kills Vivaldi.

The street is still deserted so Frazer and Loraine leave the body in the alley and go into the shabby café. They ask for Venizelos and the waiter goes to get him. Just as they are wondering if they have walked into a trap the waiter returns and takes them to another room, where they are welcomed by Kramer.

Though Frazer is still suspicious, Kramer reassures them and takes them to an upstairs room where they find Guy Melvin.

Guy has lost weight, but his health seems unimpaired. He seems very relieved to see them and says he has been having rather a rough time. He seems surprised to hear of the murder of Vivaldi, and assures them he had nothing to do with it. Then he says he is worried about Loraine's safety; this is no place for a girl.

They are anxious to know why he has disappeared and Guy begins his story by asking them if they recall the reported death of a notorious agent name Kammerman, whom he assures them is alive and in Belgrade. Kammerman had half of a plan which showed the hiding place of a large hoard of precious stones hidden in the Bavarian Alps. The other half of the plan was owned by a German named Hauser, who died after an air crash, and asked Guy to deliver his half of the plan to Kammerman. This half was concealed in a music-box.

When Guy reached Belgrade, which was Kammerman's address, he found Kammerman had disappeared. So he got in touch with D'Arcy, an old friend, told him about the music-box, and asked him to spread the report cautiously around that he had a rare music-box for sale. But Kammerman did not appear and in the meantime Vivaldi was on the scent, and he claimed to know where to find Kammerman. Guy then decided to contact Lefferts, whom he knew to be connected with British Intelligence, and arranged to send of message of reassurance, on the strap of the wristwatch to his sister, knowing that she would be worried about him.

Loraine points out that the watch did not come direct to her but was sent to Ross. Frazer asks for the wording of the message on the watch strap and Guy says it was to the effect that he would be out of circulation for a while, but that he was perfectly safe. When they tell Guy what was on the watch strap when it arrived he is completely mystified. Loraine produces the watch, and Guy at once detects that the strap has been changed. Frazer immediately realises the implication of this – that Kammerman, having been reported dead, has murdered the real Lefferts, assumed his identity, and – after substituting a watch strap bearing a misleading message – sent the watch to Ross hoping to put British Intelligence on the wrong scent. This would also explain why Kammerman (in the guise of Lefferts) had later suggested to Frazer and Loraine that Nis should be the centre for investigations; another attempt to get them away from the danger spot.

Miss Rowley, the British agent who had been sent by Ross as a cover to keep an eye on Frazer and Loraine, had immediately suspected Kammerman when she saw him posing as Lefferts, so she followed him to D'Arcy's pet shop, where he murdered her.

Kammerman (still disguised as Lefferts, of course) has invited Loraine to dinner to that they can discuss her brother's disappearance more fully, and Frazer and Kramer proceed to make plans to ensure that Kammerman shall not escape. Frazer suggests that Loraine puts her cards on the table, tells Kammerman that she has found Guy and is prepared to do a deal over the music-box. If he agrees, she is to ask him to accompany her back to the Flaming Torch.

172

Guy is doubtful whether Kammerman will fall for the idea, but they eventually agree that it is worth trying.

**

Next night, at the hotel, D'Arcy watches the entrance, then phones through to Frazer's room that Kammerman has arrived. Frazer tells Loraine that as soon as she leaves for the café, he and D'Arcy will be in close attendance.

When Loraine tells Kammerman over dinner that she has found her brother, he is apparently very surprised. She then asks him what he is prepared to pay for the music-box. He pretends not to know what she is talking about, but she then challenges his identity as Lefferts and says she knows he is really Kammerman. She tells him her brother wants 200,000 dollars for the music-box. He agrees to go with her to the café and talk to Guy.

D'Arcy and Frazer follow Kammerman's car and keep it in sight. However, they do not know that Kammerman has drugged Loraine's coffee and she realises he is not making for the café after all.

In the car behind, Frazer realises there's something wrong and asks D'Arcy to overtake the other car. As they go round a traffic island, Kammerman shoots and punctures a tyre on D'Arcy's car. Kammerman then continues right round the island and doubles back on his tracks. Then Frazer and D'Arcy realise that Loraine has been abducted.

Frazer gets back to the café and breaks the news to Guy, who wants to contact the police at once. But Kramer restrains him, pointing out that the music-box is still the master card and that Kammerman is sure to get in touch very soon. Presently, Kammerman telephones and puts Loraine on the line. She begs Frazer to see that Guy hands over the music-box. Kammerman comes back on the line and assures Frazer nothing will happen to Loraine if his instructions are followed.

He says he wants Guy Melvin to deliver the music-box to 214 Skopje Boulevard, where a girl named Maxime will be waiting to receive it. If this is carried out immediately Loraine will be returned to the café.

Kramer suggests they raid the house, but Frazer points out that Kammerman will not be there; nor will Loraine. Then Kramer has the idea of tracing the telephone call.

He achieves this after some coercion of a girl friend at the telephone exchange. The call had come from the Villa Constantine in the mountains about twenty miles away. It is now an entertainment centre run by an American exile, Mrs Decker.

***

At the Villa, Kammerman's plan precipitates a quarrel between himself and Loraine and he slaps her face. Mrs Decker comes in, and Kammerman tells her that Maxime will be bringing the music-box, on receipt of which he will pay Mrs Decker 10,000 dollars.

Frazer arrives at the Villa Constantine, accompanied by D'Arcy, Guy Melvin, and Kramer. They enter the open air restaurant without arousing any suspicion, leaving D'Arcy to stay with the car. Frazer goes off to reconnoitre, while the other two stay at the table. He encounters Mrs Decker, but she does not know him and directs him back to the restaurant.

He returns to the others to report that there must be over twenty rooms. Guy is impatient and wants to make a thorough search, but Kramer thinks it would be better to wait for the big musical diversion to begin. This, he knows, tends to get noisy, with fireworks, etc.

Loraine is sleeping when Mrs Decker returns to her room to report to Kammerman that there is a stranger wandering around. She describes Frazer and Kammerman recognises him. He decides that Loraine must be got away at once and Mrs Decker suggests he take her to the chalet a mile away. He says he will wait until a noisy dance is in progress. Then he wakes Loraine to tell her about the new plan. Her brother, he says, has insisted on her being returned to the hotel before he will hand over the music-box. Having delivered her there, Kammerman will go to the café to collect the box. She gives him her word that she will not try to escape on the way back to Belgrade.

At the height of the carnival Frazer hears a shot outside. D'Arcy comes pushing his way through the crowd to tell them he tried to stop Kammerman taking Loraine away, but he was shot in the shoulder. D'Arcy tells them the direction, and Frazer and Guy Melvin go off in pursuit.

In Kammerman's car Loraine tries to get possession of the wheel and make him stop, for she realises that she has been tricked. They approach a narrow bridge over a ravine. The car swerves into the parapet and crashes; she is thrown clear on to a bank. Kammerman is trapped in his seat and killed. Loraine is slightly injured, but Guy and Frazer arrive in time to take her to hospital. They search Kammerman and find the other half of the plan in his wallet.

***

Frazer goes to see Loraine in hospital and tells her that Ross has now investigated the complete plan and he (Frazer) is to go to Salzenhoff to recover the jewels. He says he hates the idea of leaving her there; she assures him Guy will take good care of her. Besides, she has had some good news – a letter from her husband.

Frazer is taken aback and asks why she never mentioned her husband before. She says they had been separated for over a year. Her husband had heard some rumours about her being in danger and had written to say he was worried; also to suggest that they might give their marriage another chance. Furthermore, he will fly over and fetch her home as soon as she is well enough.

She notices that Frazer is absorbed in his thoughts and asks him what is on his mind. He is deciding, he says, whether he can get the evening plane to Vienna.

THE END

Press Pack

press cuttings about Tim Frazer and the Melynfforest Mystery ...

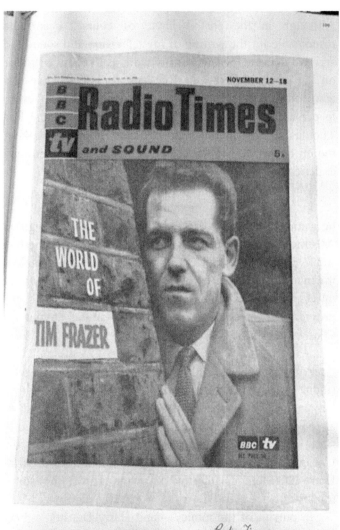

The World of Tim Frazer by **Francis Durbridge**

Shortly after the production of my last tv serial *The Scarf* I started planning the Tim Frazer series; creating the characters and developing the whole eighteen episodes which comprise the three separate Tim Frazer adventures. Although in the past I have, of course, been solely responsible for the writing of my television and sound radio serials I decided, because of my work as Executive Producer on the series, that it was necessary for me to have script associates on *The World of Tim Frazer*. I was lucky enough to persuade two top tv playwrights, Clive Exton and Barry Thomas, together with novelist Charles Hatton, to work with me on the writing of the episodes. It was a new and happy experience.

What kind of man is Tim Frazer?

Let me start by saying that he is not a private eye. Nor is he a tough, gimmicky, trigger-happy, dame-slapping, mid-Atlantic character of no fixed abode. He is, to be perfectly frank, rather like the chap you met the other day. You know the man I mean – the fellow who arrived late for the theatre, upset your daughter's chocolates, borrowed your programme, and then – to crown it all – smiled at your wife. (Yes, of course she smiled back; Tim Frazer's that sort of character.)

After being educated at a minor English public school (didn't do frightfully well, I'm afraid, except for languages,) Frazer spent four years in the Middle East with an engineering company, finally returning to England to start a small machine-tool business of his own. Unfortunately, the firm went broke, and Frazer's partner, Harry Denston, disappeared – owing Tim a fair sum of money.

In pursuit of the money – and Harry Denston – Frazer suddenly finds himself engaged in a considerably more hazardous and dangerous occupation than engineering. (*Editor's note: Read the volume The World of Tim Frazer*).

I am delighted that the part of Tim Frazer is to be played by the excellent actor Jack Hedley; and that Alan Bromly, who has been associated with my previous serials, will be producing the first, and that the second and third adventures are to be produced by Terence Dudley and Richmond Harding. The three complete stories covered by *The World of Tim Frazer* move swiftly through a variety of backgrounds as widely contrasted as Amsterdam and Tiger Bay.

Radio Times

Weeks of Hard Work For Jack

Jack Hedley lowered himself gingerly on to a hard, shabby couch in one of those out-of-the-way halls in London where the BBC rehearses its programmes

He had a badly bruised hip, the result of falling too realistically over a couch in *The World of Tim Frazer*. But, as every actor knows, if you don't do a thing realistically on television, it shows.

Altogether, Tim Frazer has given Hedley the most strenuous four months of his life, not excluding his time in the Royal Navy. When this Francis Durbridge serial finishes next month he will have appeared every Tuesday evening for eighteen weeks in a live production.

"What has made this serial doubly hard work," said Jack Hedley, "is that we have been filming and rehearsing at the same time. Normally all the filming for exteriors is done before rehearsals start. It has meant that sometimes I have had to learn parts from an episode five weeks ahead at the same time as the current episode."

It can be very confusing but fortunately he has a photographic memory and has no difficulty in memorising lines.

Neither does hard work bother this 31-year-old actor. "I like it," he said.

Nevertheless, he is looking forward to the one week's holiday which is sandwiched in between the end of the Frazer marathon and the start of rehearsals for a play which opens at the Arts Theatre, London, in April.

Provisional title for the play is *Nobody But The Chickens*, and it is by James Doran, son of Lesley Storm. In it he will play a journalist dissatisfied by his work.

After only three and a half years as an actor the world of Jack Hedley looks very promising.

Tim Frazer has brought him recognition but fortunately, he said, people still call him Mr Hedley and not Mr Frazer.

He is also paying one of the penalties of television success – a fan mail of 200 to 300 letters a week to be dealt with.

Tim Frazer Off At A Cracking Good Pace
Tim Frazer is off on the BBC on the third and last of his ventures into the world of danger and mystery.

The pace is the fastest yet by author Francis Durbridge.

A whiff of exotic perfume, a snatch of a Welsh folk song captured on tape, a body in the woods, murder – these are some of the ingredients of what already promises to be the best of the three cases.

Jack Hedley is a fine choice for the title role. His cool portrayal of the tough but clever Tim has built him into the image of a new-type of hero who, I am sure, will be copied often on television.

Also distinguishing himself in the series, after first night lapses, Ralph Michael, the Shakespearean actor, who plays

Charles Ross, head of the Secret Service branch that employs Frazer.

Top Marks For Thrill Technique

Trust thriller writer Francis Durbridge – he first produces a turn up for the book in *The World of Tim Frazer* in unmasking ******** as the unknown Ericson, head of the diamond smuggling organisation. Then he whisked us straight into another serial adventure and suspense, with Tim off on a strange assignment in Wales.

The familiar Durbridge technique of producing tension with telephone calls was reinforced last night by a tape recorder and a mysterious tape of a Welsh folk song. Tim Frazer's world is certainly no dull place.

Aberdeen Press and Journal

Busy Tim

The World of Tim Frazer still dangles us tight in the noose of suspense and speculation.

Busy Tim's got another body to frown over. Quite an attractive woman but rather spoiled by a knife in her back. No wonder Busy Tim always looks sort of melancholy.

Tuesday's Man

Tim Frazer, Tuesday's man with a nose for trouble, is all set for a crashing finale next week. There's an awful lot to be sorted out when Tim gets out of the tight corner he's heading for at the moment. I liked the follow-up to last week's cliff-hanger about the overcoat. Nothing so corny as something concealed in the lining in a Durbridge story. His twist to establish a time and an identity was masterly.

Glasgow Evening Times

A Poser For The Fireside Detectives

The master craftsman of the tele-thriller, Francis Durbridge, has set millions of amateur detectives their hardest problem of all with the third and last of his Tim Frazer stories for the BBC.

Almost everyone in the cast, except Frazer himself, and the two dead women, could turn out to be the master mind in this espionage and murder nerve-wrecker.

My short list of suspects, in order of priority, are Dr Norman Vincent, Elwyn Roberts and Roger Thornton.

Or could it be a girl again? The only one around is Rita Coleman.

Frazer, played cool and tough by Jack Hedley, seems about to be killed. If that is to be his fate, Durbridge will raise a storm like that caused when Doyle tried to write off Sherlock Holmes.

It's elementary, my dear Watson. We want more Frazer stories.

Western Daily Mail and Bristol Mirror

Rough Going For Smooth Sleuth

The longest cliff-hanger since Pearl White's silent film sagas ends this week on BBC television. I mean, of course, *The World of Tim Frazer*. And every clue is thriller writer Francis Durbridge's own work.

But it is not such a nonchalant world as Jack Hedley, who plays the name part, would like 9,000,000 viewers to believe each week.

On the screen he lingers over a cigarette, a truly smooth sleuth. But the moment the camera turns away he hurtles across studio to the serial's next set.

Four-minute miler Herb Elliott would be impressed by his speed and stamina.

I called at the studio, armed with a stopwatch, to check a few clues about Hedley's progress. The moment I walked in a dashing young man fled past me.

Hedley himself. I waved. A sheepskin coat was left, draped across my outstretched arm.

I tried to catch him up, but he was already talking to a very shady character. They were in a café at Tiger Bay, one of eight different sets slapped against each other in the studio.

He finished his dialogue. The camera rolled towards another scene.

I held out his coat, but Hedley ran to two men, waiting the wrong side of the lens.

Nobody spoke. One man skinned a jacket from Hedley. The other folded a camel coat over his arm. A continuity girl gave him a half-smoked cigarette.

And Hedley was off again, sprinting into an office. When the camera turned his way he was casually dangling a leg over a desk.

He delivered another snatch of dialogue. The camera turned a blind eye. He leapt to my side, with breath to spare.

"This," he grimaced, "is what's put my face on the tv map, but it's murder, sheer murder, every instalment."

He didn't hear my reply. He'd leapt a dozen yards across the studio. He was supposed to be in a car driving down a country lane. That's what you saw at home.

But the car couldn't move an inch. It had neither bonnet or wheels.

The driver's seat was perched on half a dozen stout springs. A man out of camera range was rocking them. The passing scenery came from a film projected behind the car.

Then came the credit titles. Hedley's week's work was over. He shivered, croaked and announced he had flu.

"I couldn't miss this instalment because there's no such thing as an understudy in television," he gasped. "But I feel dreadful."

This poses the biggest cliff-hanger of all : will Jack Hedley's temperature drop sufficiently to let him make a final appearance on Tuesday?

Don't fail to tune in, folks, for the answer to the most spine-tingling problem given to author Durbridge.

New Type

The World of Tim Frazer, BBC's 18-episode thriller, which ends tomorrow night, is, perhaps, the most ambitious and successful feature of its kind ever to be shown on television.

Jack Hedley's skilful creation of an entirely new type of hero in the shape of a fairly conventional, humane and completely unassuming man behaving in an almost believable manner, is a fine achievement.

I can already hear the curtain calls of applause and the shouts of "encore".

An encore there certainly should be.

Bath Chronicle and Herald

One Worry In The World of Tim Frazer by James Green

Congratulations today to the BBC, master story-spinner Francis Durbridge, and the fictional Tim Frazer – who prefers to take his kudos as Jack Hedley.

The triumvirate can relax in triumph after tonight when the 18-part serial *The World of Tim Frazer* comes to an end.

Viewers have thoroughly enjoyed the weekly hokum and Jack Hedley's personal mail has been running at 300 letters a week.

Even the suspenseful Mr Durbridge admits guardedly that the serial has been his most successful.

More important, the BBC has shown to the rest of the world that it is possible to screen crime and mystery without an excess of violence.

Still, Tim Frazer has had his moments. Over the weeks he's survived such pleasantries as bangs-on-the-head, threats, a shooting, and dives over furniture.

Now, the 4,000-dollar question is: will there be another Tim Frazer epic? Nobody will say for certain.

The BBC would like more but Durbridge says it would depend on his having enough time to work on detailed preparations. And Jack Hedley is worried that he might become "typed".

Francis Durbridge has yet to write a bad tv serial and is well-known to radio audiences as the author of "Paul Temple."

Hedley has finished the series fighting off an attack of flu and on Thursday will leave for a short holiday in Portofino.

The World of Tim Frazer is the longest serial ever mounted by BBC-tv. In my opinion Frazer will be back.

But Durbridge will first have to be free of other writing commitments. There is no chance of that immediately as he is already working on a Tim Frazer … book.

Evening News

Tim's Life Was So Mixed Up

The BBC's longest running serial *The World of Tim Frazer* ends tonight after eighteen of the most successful weeks of television.

For the viewers the serial has meant nine hours of viewing, but for the serial's star, Jack Hedley, it has meant five months work.

He says: "At one time things became so involved that I was in four episodes at the same time: one about to go on the air, one in rehearsal and filming on two going on in the mornings."

Tim Frazer has helped to create a new type of tv hero … a reasonably ordinary man in the street.

But ordinary things don't seem to happen to Tim Frazer.

Daily Sketch

Looking

The World of Tim Frazer ends tonight. It is the longest ever serial put out by BBC Television. And, judging by the popular reaction, one of the most successful. Eighteen weeks have gone by since viewers were first introduced to Francis Durbridge's unusually human hero, Tim Frazer. For Jack Hedley, in the title part, it has meant some twenty weeks of work, with ten weeks of filming time interwoven with rehearsals and transmissions. The actor's comment on the character he portrays is: "Frazer has gone through quite a lot." Viewers will doubtless regard this as a modest assessment of the duties Jack has been called upon to perform.

Morning Advertiser

BBC by Jon Balor

Tonight the last of the three stories in *The World of Tim Frazer* brings to an end a very enjoyable series, expertly written by Francis Durbridge and Charles Hatton. They provided engrossing thriller material against an almost leisurely and highly civilised background, with little or no violence and well-developed characters. The production has style and polish, and the overall acting standard was excellent. But most of the credit for the success of the stories must go to Jack Hedley, who created Tim Frazer so brilliantly. How refreshing and impressive is the quiet understatement of his acting compared with the brashness and mock heroics of so many actors playing investigators on the screen today.

Tim's World Comes To An End by Tom Goldie

The world comes to an end on the BBC tonight. *The World of Tim Frazer*, at any rate, the Francis Durbridge adventures which have been running every Tuesday for the past eighteen weeks.

And for some viewers the end of the series WILL be just about the end of the world. I can recall only one other thriller series which has had such a faithful following – the *Quatermass* stories on the same channel.

The secret of Tim Frazer was that each of his instalments left several "hang-over" questions to be answered in the next one – usually such intriguing questions that the viewers just had to tune in again the following week.

More than once during the series viewers have telephoned me on Wednesday mornings to find out what had happened in the previous night's instalment, which they had missed – always for reasons beyond their control.

Actor Jack Hedley has certainly been through the mill in the course of the three adventure stories which made up *The World of Tim Frazer*. No matter what happens tonight I can't see him being killed off in the last few minutes – Tim Frazer is bound to return some day.

Glasgow Evening Times

Teleview by Denis Thomas

Tim Frazer is off to the South of France for two weeks' leave (surely he deserved a bit longer) and the Tuesday night serial takes a rest. It can be counted one of the best of Francis Durbridge's polished thrillers.

It is appropriate that Frazer, once aboard the aeroplane, should click with an attractive young French girl bound for San Tropez.

His adventures in the service of the formidable Ross give him no chance to combine business with pleasure. In Durbridge-land, you never know if a pretty girl with a nice smile is hiding a cosh in her handbag.

The success of the series owes much to Jack Hedley, who has a nice cool acting style that exactly fits the part.

Apart from the hand-tooled plot, the serial has also scored heavily in the visual impact. It has given us interesting things and places to look at. This should be a truism of all television, but it is surprising how constantly it is overlooked.

Move Heaven and Hell

After 17 intriguing weeks the Tim Frazer saga galloped to its end and we must now be unduly curious and ask how secret service chief Ross knew so many of the answers. Neither must we question the reporter's most fortuitous intervention and other improbabilities, for this has been a splendid hunt and not a week too long either. Occasionally the BBC conceives things on a grand scale, as it did with this serial, and has received much public approbation on its enterprise. The Corporation should move heaven and hell to secure Mr Durbridge and Mr Frazer to add zest to the programmes next winter.

Nottingham Evening News

Tim Frazer's World by Miss J. V. Pollard (reader's letter)

I would like to express my appreciation to all those concerned in the production of *The World of Tim Frazer*, especially the scriptwriters for the original dialogue and the unconventional approach to crime detection.

I am sure many viewers who have enjoyed this eighteen-week thriller would appreciate a repeat showing of the whole or part, preferably at a later hour in the evening or at the weekend, as (like myself) they may have missed several of the episodes.

Radio Times

Looking For More

The World of Tim Frazer, the BBC's longest tv serial, came to an end with a flourish after 18 episodes, split into three stories.

Many will be looking for more, as Francis Durbridge succeeded in getting dramatic action and coherent adventures into a satisfying whole. Jack Hedley, the young actor in the title role, contributed to the success of the serial by the diffident way in which he played it.

Derby Evening Telegraph

We Should See More Of Frazer

So it's all over. Tim Frazer, the man whose exploits have become a Tuesday night "must" for millions of viewers and whose personality has made him the idol of every woman viewer of my acquaintance last night concluded his probe into dirty work in South Wales.

But as we watched him dating a pretty girl as he flew to the South of France for a well-earned rest, I felt that we'd probably be seeing more of Mr Frazer … providing actor Jack Hedley doesn't mind being almost certainly "typed".

Certainly, we can expect more mystery from Francis Durbridge's fertile brain. But without Hedley, there'll never be another Frazer.

Although this BBC serial had a run of 18 episodes, it nevertheless ended last night at a gallop, covering more ground in the final half-hour than two or three earlier episodes put together.

And I'm still wondering just how Frazer's angling colleague earned his salary on this Welsh assignment.

Liverpool Echo

Tim Frazer Has Earned A Good Holiday
The BBC's marathon Tim Frazer serial – eighteen episodes of it, ended in the manner of all the best thriller films, with one of those spectacular pursuits of the wanted man which usually involve rooftops or railway junctions.

For good measure, this fine old fling in the arduous life of Mr Frazer included both the rooftops and the railway lines. The quarry escaped, of course, staggering breathlessly into the cabin of the ship which was to take him to freedom.

And there, of course, sitting on the bunk was the invincible Mr Frazer, with a gun and a cynical smile.

He has earned his holiday. Since he became one of television's most popular characters a few months ago, he has given secret service fiction its biggest fillip in years.

The series has also been a splendid success for actor Jack Hedley. His slow-speaking, slightly-worried version of a super-secret agent has been a pleasant change from the more usual, slick-talking linx-eyed variety, beloved of television writers, with an eye on the transatlantic market.

You may call this sort of thing the purest hooey. You might be right. Or, at least, you might be partly right. But if you don't find it greatly entertaining, then you should try more green vegetables in your diet.

Liverpool Daily Post

Television Review by **Mary Crozier** (contains spoilers)

The last episode of *The World of Tim Frazer* last night brought a rapid succession of escapes and life or death chases that made a brilliant end to a crime serial that had slowly but surely tightened its grip through, in all, three stories and 18 instalments. The last story has been the best, partly because the setting in the Welsh countryside has added an out-of-doors breath of fresh air to the innumerable car journeys which are a necessary part of crime and detection.

The character of Tim Frazer, played by Jack Hedley, has grown gradually stronger and more interesting. This is the super-secret service agent, cool, aloof, sulky, always giving the impression he doesn't know where he is and might be on the other side. It is typical that his boss at headquarters says, even in the last episode, "Does Frazer know the full story yet?" Whether Frazer knew the full story or not, he dealt with events magnificently in this last episode, chasing his man across innumerable ledges and roofs and finally anticipating him in the cabin of the ship on which he was escaping. I record with some satisfaction that I had noted Roberts, the mild man who played gramophone records, as the suspect from the start; but this was merely through television intuition, an acquired capacity and a tribute in its way to the educative powers of the small screen.

The Guardian

How Times Have Changed by **Peter Quince**

Well, Tim Frazer made it, didn't he? All the bad boys and girls neatly sorted out in eighteen weekly instalments and then off to the South of France for a holiday.

I gather that the BBC are well satisfied with the experiment of running this three-part serial over four and a half months – and that there is some prospect of seeing Frazer again next autumn.

This news should please all! Francis Durbridge fans – and, of course, all Frazer fans. I had heard that he had made quite a hit with the girls, and I was able to confirm this with some on-the-spot market research. Not quite a flaming heartthrob in the Adam Faith – Cliff Richard class, I gather, but "definitely very attractive – and nice, if you know what I mean".

Indeed, I do – but how times have changed! No one, I fancy, would ever have described Bulldog Drummond or The Saint as "nice" – and yet Frazer's niceness and his boy-you-might-have-seen-on-the-bus-if-you-were-terribly-lucky appeal has no doubt helped to build up the popularity of the series. But the trouble with eighteen weeks on the trot (and the possibility of another stint in the autumn) means that it is now very difficult to imagine Jack Hedley in any other role. I see him doom from here to eternity to this hair-raising round of spy-busting – unless, of course, he eases himself into Ross's place behind that big desk and sends other lads out on deeds of derring-do.

Congratulations to all concerned in this mystery marathon. It has been smoothly and entertainingly presented and has gained immensely from the special gloss-finish that the BBC slap so expertly on its productions of this sort – and which rival firms achieve only spasmodically.

Huddersfield Daily Examiner

Window display – Foyle's bookshop – London – 1962

Window display – Foyles Bookshop
London 1962

Printed in Great Britain
by Amazon